LOW PASTURES

LOW PASTURES

Bill James

SEVERN
HOUSE

First world edition published in Great Britain and the USA in 2022
by Severn House, an imprint of Canongate Books Ltd,
14 High Street, Edinburgh EH1 1TE.

Trade paperback edition first published in Great Britain and the USA in 2023
by Severn House, an imprint of Canongate Books Ltd.

severnhouse.com

British Library Cataloguing-in-Publication Data
A CIP catalogue record for this title is available from the British Library.

ISBN-13: 978-1-4483-0572-8 (cased)
ISBN-13: 978-1-4483-0574-2 (trade paper)
ISBN-13: 978-1-4483-0573-5 (e-book)

All Severn House titles are printed on acid-free paper.

Typeset by Palimpsest Book Production Ltd.,
Falkirk, Stirlingshire, Scotland.
Printed and bound in Great Britain by
TJ Books, Padstow, Cornwall.

ONE

O
ccasionally, the plain, matter-of-fact names for certain bits of the city gave Detective Chief Superintendent Colin Harpur true and deep delight. It happened now, despite the deado lying prone quite close, his skull shattered by at least two shots from behind, in Harpur's admittedly hurried estimate. Plentiful blood across the rear neck and shoulders of the victim seemed to confirm Harpur's judgement, and so did the dead man's cultured light grey wool suit, now patchily stained on the back. Harpur was alone with the body. He'd been told about it by one of those secretive, confidential whispers that detection depended on.

'Sand and gravel wharf' was the official label for this stretch of docklands. It struck Harpur as perfect. Dredging vessels came in on the tide from the channel through the lock gates and took their place alongside the wharf to unload cargoes of sand or gravel, or a mixture, sucked up mechanically through a wide pipe from the sea bottom where it had hung about for centuries, a lot of centuries. Now, or soon after, it would get transformed into cement. Harpur liked this notion – its purposefulness: the sand would help construct houses, schools, headstones, office blocks, jails, motorways, multi-storey car parks, perhaps good enough to last a couple of lifetimes, or a good many more lifetimes than this corpse's. OK, that didn't sound very long when compared with the sand's slow grind-down creation, but it was not nothing.

A dredger like this one here now would cough up its pre-ordered offering – sand or gravel or mix – from the minor depths and this seemed to Harpur neat, tidy, logical. It had natural sequences. He saw beauty, also. For instance, 'carapace' was a word he reckoned could be quite reasonably used about the outer covering of a gravel grain. At daytime, if the sun shone, this carapace might glint brilliantly, beautifully for a while. Sand was different; it gave no glint whatever the weather.

Sand in a pile on the wharf looked only serviceable, as though it had a job to do and would do it, adding itself to the cement powder in due proportion.

Because the dead man had been shot from behind he had pitched forward when hit, throwing his hands and arms ahead of himself on the ground, and the sleeves of his jacket were slightly pulled back in this collapse. He had on his left wrist what looked to Harpur like a very elegant and pricey simple-faced watch. It was secured by a brown leather strap, not one of those gold or silver jobs glowering like a fetter. The combination of modesty and wealth made Harpur think this must be someone from outside the area. He was pushed towards such a wider view as locals didn't often, in his experience, favour understatement.

Now and then, when Harpur dealt with a murder, he got the idea that this particular death had meaning well beyond the ordinary and obvious. The feeling certainly did not arise with every murder case, but when it did the impression for Harpur was always very strong. And so it turned out now, with this splendidly dressed white male on the wharf floor at almost dawn. The soles of his nicely polished black shoes showed next to no wear. Harpur believed shoe soles could often tell a tale.

Harpur found himself thinking hard that this execution had a special, urgent and possibly widespread message. God, the flapdoodle term 'overtones' had somehow got into his brain: did this crumpled, very tastefully dressed clutter on the floor really have overtones? Often, someone talking about a murder might say, 'this killing surely hints at something', and Harpur would have replied: 'yes it hints at no circulation, no oxygen, no life.' Today he regarded that as stupidly negative, glib and useless. The present fatality probably spoke a warning, or more than one, and he knew he'd better listen hard and respectfully to its silent swansong.

Because the victim had apparently crumpled to the left, Harpur could see only part of his face on the floor and didn't recognize it. Harpur was good on faces. He crouched to be nearer. The man's jacket had been unbuttoned, and part of it lay spread out flat on the ground from under the body. Harpur enjoyed a hearty snuffle in the area of lining exposed there. It was like being wrapped in a friendly wall. Lingering darkness helped. Harpur admired the tailor's bright skill – he, or she, had made the jacket's lining resemble the oblong greystone of a formidable building, perhaps a jail.

Harpur lying close to the gaudy remains, could feel the hard bulk of a pistol over the man's left breast. The lining was too heavy for him to recognize by touch the make of weapon, possibly an automatic, and not an imitation. This guesswork severely pestered Harpur while he was on his hands and knees touring the dead man, trying to keep clear of the scattered blood and fragments and to decide absolutely from a greater closeness how many bullets had shattered the skull, two or three. He acknowledged that, in a way, this kind of post-mortem accountancy was fairly superfluous because the man was dead and the number of bullets that killed him didn't much matter. Harpur's training edged him towards thoroughness, though, and he didn't fight it.

In any case, he wanted to make an estimate of what the face might have looked like before being ripped by the double, and possibly triple, exit damage – back of the neck, maybe part of the jaw, then the nose. As far as Harpur could make out by a good stare at the former face, it definitely wasn't somebody he knew, either through the job or personally. Half a nose taken away, as here, made a difference. It wasn't just a missing nostril. The whole layout and balance of his features were affected. Harpur guessed that even close relatives might have had trouble recognizing him, if he had any. Harpur called in to headquarters and reported the find.

He took as good a grip as he could manage and gently drew the pistol from its shoulder-harness. As he thought, an automatic, a Walther. From its weight he guessed it to be fully loaded. He held it out in front of him, thrilled by its smooth lines. How elegant and shapely automatics were, in contrast to revolvers.

There was a sudden insulting yell: 'Grand pose, Col. Suits you,' Iles said. He had approached around the stern of the dredger.

Harpur decided the assistant chief must have an informant

network as good as Harpur's; perhaps better. Although it was
2 a.m., Iles had taken the time to dress formally in one of his
silver-buttoned blazers, well-ironed shirts and hockey-club
tie. He was a keen playing member, strong in attack from the
right wing.

Iles's arrival reinforced Harpur's belief that the shooting
was most probably more than itself, and the beginning of
something extraordinary; something not altogether good,
perhaps not remotely good and sickeningly bad, in fact.

An assistant chief constable didn't normally attend a run-
of-the-mill slaughter aftermath. But normality was not one of
the ACC's glistening talents. He would probably recognize the
normal if he met it, but would decide this was no fun and not
for him, thanks. Or, he had his own notion of what normal
looked like, and not everyone agreed.

He could sense and sniff potentially major bother and he'd
need to scrutinize it. So, here he was, svelte and gleaming in
his lovely gear. Effortlessly, and at once, he got down on all
fours with Harpur. This, Harpur realized, was not warm-
hearted, simple matiness. To make sure he didn't get left
behind, Iles would place himself to see anything Harpur
might discover. The ACC had a constant, raging, extremely
warranted fear that Harpur would hold information back from
him so that Harpur, not Iles, would control an investigation
and pick up any kudos for resolving it.

Depending on what you knew of their background and
history, you could decide the way Iles and Harpur worked
harmoniously together on the body and clothing that they
must be close, cheery, long-term pals, used to sharing a job
and always ready to do it. But this would be about as wrong
as you could get: life was not like that; not these lives, at any
rate. Each dreaded with a miserable, undying intensity the
possibility that the other might discover something unique
and crucial to one of their projects and leave the other
looking eternally inept and null.

Iles, especially, had a lot to lose. At his rank – almost top
rank – he ought to brave a confrontation with wettish sand in
a heap only as long as it brought more clear credit and
gloire to his name. And Harpur didn't see how this cock-crow

dockside episode could boost the ACC. Rumour said he might be thinking about trying for a full chief post – not a mere assistant role – at a police force elsewhere, and he would need to be careful to keep his reputation sound.

Harpur wished intently that the Iles hadn't turned up today. There was the matter of his roaming wife. Although Sarah Iles seemed to have settled contentedly into motherhood since the birth of their second child, some while back she'd suffered episodes of deep, very proactive sexual unrest. Harpur had tried to help. It was over. There was Denise now. But when Iles and Harpur were forced into exceptionally close contact by the job, it could still lead to notable stress and unpleasantness initiated by the ACC, and not at all now to do with the murder. Some who had known about Sarah Iles and Harpur thought it continued, would not believe it had finished.

'Ah,' Iles said.

'I thought this death might interest you, sir,' Harpur replied heartily, emptily. 'Very much up your as-it-were street. As you see, terrific suit including waistcoat. We don't come across many of those about lately.'

'We've had this kind of situation once or twice before haven't we, Col?' Iles said.

'Have we, sir?' They had. Harpur remembered the occasions well. It was why he felt so troubled now.

'Oh, yes,' Iles said.

Oh, hell. 'I haven't been able to identify him or get a background,' Harpur replied.

'That's not what I mean,' Iles said.

Harpur had known it wasn't what he meant. Yes, there was the matter of the ACC's wife. 'I wondered if this savagery here had implications outside the immediate,' Harpur said, seeking a diversion, any diversion.

'The immediate,' Iles said. 'How exactly does the immediate look to you, Harpur? What is the immediate?'

'Well, the body. The murder.'

'And what is "outside" this immediate?' Iles said.

'The more general picture. Does it tell us about that?'

'Which more general picture?'

'We have to learn something from this dead man,' Harpur replied.

'Learn what?' Iles asked. He pulled out the necktie of the corpse. It was blue and grey striped and genuine silk. Iles leaned forward, rubbed his right cheek appreciatively on it. 'Pleasant,' he said. 'There's a bit of body warmth still present. One should always spend that small amount extra for quality.'

'It's as if the tie knew you'd be along and waited,' Harpur said.

'You taking the piss?' Iles said. 'Let's switch topics, shall we? Can we talk about my wife? As I said, we're into repeats. I'm sure I've asked a certain type of question previously but let's revisit, OK?'

'Whatever you wish, sir.'

'Tell me, do you think, Harpur, that in any other British police force, or indeed, police forces throughout the world, an assistant chief constable (Operations) might be at the site of an undoubted homicide and find he is in the company of an officer, subordinate officer, who has adulterously had his wife, and who might be confidentially savouring the memory of it though his attention should be entirely on the very present casualty. Do you want a rub of this?' he said, offering the tie.

'Nothing in his pockets. Systematically cleaned out post-death, I'd say,' Harpur replied. Except, of course, it was no reply to what Iles had asked, but Harpur would profoundly like to get off the blistering Sarah theme. 'Possibly yourself, sir, can help with identification. That would be an advance. I've no ideas.'

'Sarah and I chew over it, that unsplendid fling,' Iles said. Like Harpur, the ACC moved carefully so as not to get messed up near the incomplete head. 'There's no festering secrecy in my home. She regrets it all – regrets the past error. Sarah is like that. She will admit mistakes. She is even-handed. You may have heard of jot-and-tittles, Col. Well, the dismissive attitude she has currently towards you is total, all jots, all tittles wiped out.'

Iles began to shout across the murdered man at Harpur.

'You might think you're the one she favours more than her husband. Arrogance. Vanity. Self-delusion. You're as nothing to her, zilch, nil, void. In her memory there is a gloriously spacious blank and you are entirely it. I pity you, yes, pity.'

The full Scenes of Crime unit in masks and white dungarees had arrived, responding to Harpur's call, and waited considerately until the assistant chief completed his anguished résumé of this relationship, but now approached and began their work.

Iles lowered his tone, grew more or less sane in that famed, fast recovery fashion of his: 'We've been convinced something like this – the ruthless death – was bound to happen and soon, haven't we, Col?' he said. 'We see a kind of paradox in such an instance of thuggery, don't we? This city's success brings destructive, appalling peril. If he did but know it, this deceased is a trailblazer. It's a kind of malign pay-back, a rough touch of hubris, meaning obnoxious, doomed pride, Col.' Iles bent forward and now began to finger ecstatically the material in the left lapel of the corpse's jacket. 'A London creation, this,' Iles said. 'Brilliant ensemble, and it chimes so sweetly with his general deluxe aura, doesn't it: the tie and highest-quality non-plastic buttons?' Iles gave himself a brush down with his right hand. Harpur did the same for himself. They'd stood.

'I,' Iles said. 'Yes, I.'

'You, sir?'

'I,' Iles replied.

'In which sense, sir?' Harpur said.

'When you look at this dead man, Harpur, you see implications. Implications are all very well. But me, when I consider the corpse, I feel not implications but responsibility. That might surprise you. I mean, though, that I have made this city, this area, this bailiwick so sweet and comfy that all sorts want to come here. So many of them want it that there is deadly competition. There is violence, there is killing, there is our friend here stretched out on the wharf.'

He had finished his brushing and pointed with his right thumb at the body. 'I'm not in any way ashamed to say so. If anything, the reverse.' The use of his thumb as a pointer, rather than a finger, seemed to take away what remained of the man on the floor's dignity. It could be argued, probably, that there wasn't, in fact, much dignity left anyway for someone flattened like this, despite the distinction of his garb. Harpur thought that almost certainly if he himself was shot and lying lifeless, Iles would indicate the Harpur body in the same curt, unhysterical style.

'No shame? Right, sir? Is that your point?' Harpur replied.

'One sees an inevitability about these developments,' Iles said.

'Right, sir.'

'There were bound to be side-effects,' Iles said.

'To what sir?' Harpur asked.

'Oh yes,' Iles replied.

Harpur searched his store of vocabulary for some soft soap: 'I wouldn't be so brazen as to rush in with an interpretation of your comments, sir, but I think I do see their main thrust and respect it.'

'Thank you, thank you, thank you, I'm fucking sure,' Iles said.

'Inevitable. Exactly. Destined,' Harpur said. Iles had his own way of looking at things, not always what Harpur would have expected; possibly not always what Iles would have expected either, and he'd hit back. 'Thank you (in triplicate) I'm fucking sure,' was not a friendly response to Harpur's lame praise.

Harpur's method of dealing with Iles's occasional egomaniac outbursts was to pretend they hadn't taken place, and keep talking about something else, that is, move sideways, the same technique as he used when he and Iles talked about Sarah: escape, if escape were possible.

'How I see it, you as Operations have given this domain, sir, a serene and prosperous reputation and character through a progressive attitude on drugs, namely toleration of the trade as long as it keeps gang warfare off the streets. It's what I tried to get at when I referred to the "immediate" and "the general picture". Property values here have soared, as they have in other areas with permissive policies of that sort – Colorado in the States, for instance, I'm told. Some of the more distinguished housing on our patch has seen a rise in worth of almost a third in less than a year. I'm thinking of, say, Panicking Ralph Ember's Low Pastures. I was chatting to an estate agent recently.

'But, of course, our radiantly admirable conditions are envied by those living in less comfortable parts of the country and, yes, other countries, too. The good word about our enlightened regime is around and far reaching. Our success attracts others. People want to leave – get away from – those rough conditions and switch to here. I mean not just smokers and snorters, though there are many of those. But it's also folk who want no more than a safe, ordered and cheerful environment for themselves and their children. Brilliantly, devotedly, courageously you have helped provide that for them, sir,' Harpur said.

'Regrettably, there is a bad side to that picture of our grounds, though,' Harpur continued. 'This fine city by its very excellence makes it liable to attack and, yes, to its own possible devastation. Drugs big-fellows from elsewhere see marketing opportunities in this charming, peaceable, well-heeled community. They naturally want to establish themselves and their business here. As we've said, "inevitable". And more than one of these opportunists hopes to break into this territory. Hence, there will be, or already is, vicious competition. Is our dead stranger part of it? I think so. The property inflation is very comforting for the owners like Ralph Ember, of course. Yet, it is also unnerving. It is bound to attract money launderers, crooked gang masters, bent tycoons. We can visualize, can't we, some big villain telling one of his women, "I'll get to lie down in Low Pastures".'

Harpur knew Iles would not like this kind of plonking verbiage even if true, or especially if true. The assistant chief was sure to be infuriated by somebody who would actually say 'hence' in serious conversation, which was why Harpur had used it.

'Did you mention implications, Col?' Iles said. 'Yes, I think you might be on to something.' Now and then the ACC liked to hearten Harpur with a bit of praise. Iles had created for himself a kind of brisk aggression when dealing with Harpur. He would stick with it now. Of course, Harpur's affair with Sarah Iles made an extra reason for enmity. Anyway, whatever the reason or reasons. Iles found he couldn't rid himself of them, except very infrequently: now, for instance. This surprised him. Maybe a shift away would make him gentler.

They left the body with the Murder Squad and Harpur drove home. It was near dawn. He more or less liked this time of day – or night. It meant you had a job. Who else would be up around now? True, the job had Iles in it and his monstrous quirks, but these could be managed. Harpur had heard those rumours that the ACC might be looking for an even bigger rank elsewhere, perhaps making any discussion of how to cope with him here irrelevant.

Harpur must have woken Jill as he unlocked the front door at home. Jill, aged eleven, slept more lightly than her older sister, Hazel. Jill appeared on the landing in lightweight, blue pyjamas. Finger on his lips, Harpur signalled to her to keep quiet. From the hall Harpur tried to wave her back to bed. But he had an idea that wouldn't work. It didn't.

She came down the stairs, her face split by a couple of yawns as she neared the bottom. 'Emergency Dad?' she said. 'I mean – so late.' He lowered his finger.

'All OK,' he said, whispering.

'Yes, maybe, but so late, Dad. You're getting old for these kinds of hours – shortness of breath, blood circulation slower. A lot of research has been done on the health of the middle-aged. Do they realize the difficulties when they sent you? It's inconsiderate.'

They hadn't sent him. He'd sent himself. They hadn't known about it until he'd told them. A tipster had given him an opportunity to act solo. It had been a gross breach of rules to search the corpse and not to report the find at once. Luckily, Iles, although an ACC, went along with this kind of self-serving, devious concealment from colleagues. He might have invented it.

'What was it?' Jill said.

'What was what?'

'Being out.'

'An incident.'

'I know it must have been an incident, don't I, Dad, but what incident? Serious?'

'Well, yes, serious,' Harpur replied.

'In the death category?'

'Go back to bed now, please,' Harpur said. 'You'll disturb Hazel.'

'Was Des Iles involved?'

'Bed,' Harpur replied.

'Iles *was* involved, wasn't he?'

'Iles is ACC (Operations), so something of this sort would be bound to come his way,' Harpur said.

'Something of which sort?'

'It's sure to fall within his responsibility,' Harpur said.

'What is?'

'Incidents of this sort.'

'Which?' she asked.

'Which what?'

'Which sort?' she said.

'It's all in hand now.'

'Good,' she said. 'Is it because you were where it is?'

'Sleep, please,' Harpur replied.

After a few more minutes, Jill seemed to realize that she would learn no more from him and climbed back upstairs. There was something about the methodical way her feet dealt with the stairs that declared she was happy to have done her duty.

When he went into his bedroom, Denise, under the duvet, half awoke and reached blindly for her cigarette packet on the bedside table. Harpur pushed this to where she would be sure to reach it quickly. She had on a t-shirt he long ago used for jogging runs that she'd obviously found deep in one of the chest drawers amid a lot of forgotten-about clothes. Sometimes Denise grew very curious about Harpur's past, and she must have done a real search to find the shirt. Before going out earlier, he'd mentioned he had a call and perhaps there was something in his voice that said it was something bad, something very bad, something grave.

It pleased him in a big, big way that Denise was here. His children loved it when she stopped over, but it wasn't a surprise to him. If she'd sensed Harpur had been summoned to an especially grim event, she would want to support and comfort him. That's the kind of girl she was, though so young.

She located the cigarette packet and closed her fingers affec-
tionately around it. There was a lighter as well. She'd been
sleeping on her left side, usual for Denise. She opened one
eye and seemed to see him. She gave a small smile. A light
burned at the far end of the room.

'You're back.' That would be as much as she would say.
The hour and perhaps the tone of his voice when he went out
earlier must tell her that he'd been called to something very
troublesome. She could probably tell he was deeply shaken.
She wouldn't want to probe for details. To be near him and
full of love seemed to be enough. He was thankful. He knew
he'd slip into top-grade self-pity if he examined his reactions
to the dockside body. And self-pity would be a bit of a daft
luxury. It wasn't available to the man with half his head shot
away and his pockets cleaned out. Denise must have spotted
this frailty in Harpur. She wouldn't like it.

She moved back a couple of inches to make room for him
in the bed. She reached past Harpur and shook a cigarette
from the packet. She lit up. Harpur took the packet and the
lighter from her. She eked out the smoke in oblong sections
from her mouth and nose simultaneously, as if offering it help
to adjust to the wider environment, and could only do that if
the smoke arrived divided up into neat, well-behaved portions.

'I can stay if you want, Col.'

'I want. Do I ever not?'

Denise was an undergraduate student at the local university.
She often stopped over at Harpur's house in Arthur Street. It
wasn't every night though: Denise had a room in one of the
student blocks and spent some time there. Harpur knew she
didn't want anything too regular and/or binding with him – not
yet, at any rate. He could understand this and sympathize.
There was the matter of the age difference – her teens or
twenties, he near-forties. Denise had most of her life still to
come, some of it possibly exciting; Harpur had already seen
off a fair chunk of his, much of it dull. He'd been thinking
lately of retirement. Police pensions were very good, part paid
for by officers still serving, like Harpur.

Of course, that was not such a huge age gap. He knew of
many good relationships with similar arithmetic. Denise might

not like the prospect, though, and her parents probably wouldn't feel altogether OK about it.

He put the packet and lighter back on the table. He undressed and placed his clothes neatly on a couple of chairs. He knew he'd better be tidy in case his children, Hazel and Jill, came to welcome him later on this morning. They hated scruffiness. That made them sound prim and overbearing; the situation was not so simple, though. A while back their mother had been killed, had been murdered on a train.[1] They had an idea that as a result the household, led by Harpur, unaided, would drift into chaos and they were very vigilant for early signs. It would offend and alarm them if he left his suit and the rest of his gear on the floor. They'd wonder whether shambles had set in. The fact that the cast-off gear could indicate sexual urgency should ease their worries, perhaps. He sat on the bit of bed Denise had cleared for him, then swung his legs in and snuggled against her body. She finished the cigarette and leaned across him to crush out the stub in a saucer where there were three already.

'I've been thinking a lot about you, Col.' She was still lying across him. Her breasts felt heart-warming. This positioning made Harpur see more of the point in smoking.

'I can tell,' he said. He had a corpse with a smashed head to think about, but that was off-limits as a chat topic. Life should be about being pinned under a girl in bed if possible. Although Denise continued to give the dibby end a very thorough belabouring, she turned her head twenty degrees. 'How?' she said.

'How, what?' Harpur said.

'How could you know I've been thinking of you a lot?'

'Because I've been thinking a lot about you,' he said. 'We're like that. We match each other. No smugness, but I would expect it.'

'That's nice,' she said.

'But obvious,' Harpur said.

'Well, yes.' She was a girl being trained by the higher education system to think ruthlessly and properly, and Harpur

[1] See *Roses, Roses*.

could tell she recognized his reply as prime bullshit, not obvious at all, but felt duty-bound to keep these few minutes of babble sweet and magical. They were rare. She wouldn't get that kind of top-class smarm in her student accommodation block. Because of how she was physically stretched, and because of the smoke, her voice had become croaky. Briefly, as she dealt with the stub, her elbow was hard into his midriff. This Harpur liked. It was one of several factors that made it unique to him, too – the smoking, the smoking in bed, the intimacy, the carefully crafted conversation. A relationship ought to have rough points and they should be shared, particularized.

When she'd done convincingly for the cigarette end, then moved to sit alongside him, he could pull the t-shirt up over her head with a little help from Denise and he had his arms around her, pressing her close to him, and later so much closer. She had the lovely, happy knack of suggesting in moments like this that she desired him as much as he desired her. These young nipples spoke lovingly to him. She drew nearer, putting them chest to chest. This was something that thrilled him, especially as he knew the excitement either way was brilliantly equal, or that was how it felt to Harpur, and Harpur was no fool optimist. He'd had enough good episodes in his life to help him recognize the near-perfect, and this present moment did nearly reach that. It was worth staying up late for. When they kissed it was like a celebration, an endorsement. It had in it some of the certainty Harpur craved. It did, didn't it? He rolled further into the bed. Her body responded to him with a gentle, encompassing warmth. She no longer had the fag-end to distract her. There was a scent base but no more than faint. It had to fight hard against the smoke. It put Harpur in mind of the delicate waft that came to him when, as a child, he and his mother would gather primroses in the May sunshine.

He lay on his back with his legs apart. She got on top of him and knelt between them, placing her head and face to fondly inspect Harpur's. It seemed a good long stare and he reckoned it was full of joy and satisfaction. Her smile grew wider now and didn't at all seem short of something on account of the missing ciggie. Harpur felt pleased, though not flashily. On those past trips with the plucked primroses, he'd found the flowers lost their freshness very fast but he'd enjoyed them all the same. Same with this moment? But, surely, if she were troubled by the age business, she would not want to gaze for so long and from so near.

Harpur put up his hands and laced them together behind her head. He drew her head and face down to him so they could kiss again. He thought he felt a true and gorgeous permanence in the kiss. But didn't he always try to persuade himself into that hope when they kissed? He sought this durability by fixing his mind and eyes on to the section of her face he felt most for – Denise's brow merging with her cheek in a perfect, gentle slow drift. It was almost a curve, but Harpur wanted nothing so gaudy as jutting cheekbones. What he did want was her ever-welcome face looking down at him, or up at him, for that matter, if they were in reverse position – and they were often in reverse positions, as well as others.

Despite his gloom over what had happened at the dredger, he was still capable of wonderful joy with Denise. That was not something he'd allow himself to spell out or even think very often. Of course, there had been a life pre-Denise. He mustn't disown whatever came earlier. He thought she would understand this reluctance to talk much about the past, but he couldn't – couldn't – risk it. That might be the extreme caginess of age. As long as Denise was in the cage with him, this seemed to Harpur a reasonable compromise. The children would certainly OK it. Their approval was important because of their anxieties, though not crucial. They wouldn't expect it to be crucial, in fact would regard such a demand as stupidly destructive, blasting lovers apart.

She began to move strongly on him, keeping them locked together, him blissfully enclosed in her.

When they rested, she said: 'Do you know why I love you so much?'

'I try not to ask myself that kind of question,' he said. And this was fairly true.

'Which kind?' she said.

'The charming and marvellously promising kind,' Harpur replied.

'I like "promising",' she said. 'It's declaring there'll be a future.'

'Yes please,' Harpur said. 'No need for analysis.'

'I wondered whether you were afraid,' she said.

'Afraid of what?'

'Too much definition of where we're at – what we are to each other,' she said.

'Definition?'

'Impairment of the magic.'

'Do you think I ought to be scared?'

'I don't want you nervous and insecure, Col, I'd hate that.'

'Would you?'

'It's not how love should be, is it?'

'No. I'd hate that, too.'

'That's one of the reasons I come along – to tell you it's not, and show you it's not, regardless.'

'Regardless of what?' he said.

'Some snags,' she said. 'Difficulties. Circumstances.'

'Yes, circumstances are not totally favourable. But you're strong, Denise, you always cope.'

'I like it,' she said.

'What?'

'Coping.'

'I like it, too, that you cope. I feel safer.'

'Good, Col. Some sleep, now,' she said.

'You've had some already. You deserve it.'

'I'll get up soon and keep Hazel and Jill out while you get some more shut-eye.'

Harpur began to snore. She cuddled into him more energetically. The din told her she'd provided Harpur with a spell of peace as well as happy naked togetherness. She reckoned this was the right place for her, tucked in so comfortably against him, the noise, soothing, ugly and familiar. She felt big contentment from wearing just now his one-time jogging shirt. She had searched two chests of drawers for something crumpled like this. She wanted such an item – worn-looking, old or oldish. It might help her feel in touch with Col before she met him; in fact, most probably when she was still at school. His past intrigued her. She didn't know much about it, however. Anyone could have spotted that Harpur was more than a bit disturbed tonight. He wouldn't let her in on account of why, though. The job was like that. She wouldn't query it.

TWO

Ralph Ember, splendidly prosperous, owner of a magnificent country house and a bonny business also felt some of the fear that troubled Iles and Harpur. Perhaps it was more acute with Ralph. He had to handle it alone, didn't have a police brigade to back him if the real trouble started.

What really pissed him off was the dread that he might have helped bring about the potentially bad – potentially very bad and still worsening – changes in the commodities trade locally himself. Ralph frequently gave his own behaviour unsparing, even cruel, examination. How he was. He didn't always like what he found. In fact he only very rarely liked what he found. But he believed with a genuine, ferocious passion in absolute honesty, well . . . up to a point, that is. He could not kid himself that there was no decline in his and his family's prospects. He would have clearly liked to, but what had seemed some of his most solid assets were beginning to look like awful liabilities. They set up appallingly dangerous envy in appallingly dangerous competition.

'It's a paradox, isn't it, Ralph,' Margaret, his wife, said.

He'd decided how he was, and this was how she was. Margaret could come out with very unusual notable words like 'paradox'. A few others also had an x, but not necessarily. Although Ralph might understand them, they were words he would never speak himself in chit-chat nor hear around the clubs. For Margaret they were obviously natural, and as ready for expressing as 'and' or 'but'. Or 'expressing'.

'Paradox?' Ralph replied. 'You could put it like that.'

She could, though he couldn't. He'd been explaining to her in ordinary workaday language how things had begun to turn unpleasant – no, more than unpleasant, dangerous. That death he'd heard about was alarming, no question – a solitary visitor, extravagantly kitted out, executed on a docks wharf, and nobody inside for it, or not yet. The rumour said the man had been shot from behind, the bullet or bullets passing through the skull wall and taking away a chunk of his nose. Horrible. And found in this remote, bleak slice of the dockyard. He kept his unease to himself, though. He didn't want to scare Margaret. No need for that yet. Ralph tried never to skimp on his duty of care to Margaret and the children.

'You're excessively successful,' Margaret said, 'Toxically successful, inexorably successful.'

'That's one way to describe it,' Ralph said. Or three.

And possibly it was. Ralph thought about Low Pastures, for instance. Boon or curse? Until very recently that would have been an absurd question. It was a grand house in lovely surrounds. Nobody could question its charm and distinguished pedigree. At various times house and grounds had been owned by a lord lieutenant of the county – the monarch's personal representative hereabouts – and, in the eighteenth century, the Spanish consul lived here. There were grand moments when Ralph could get his imagination going and fancy one or other of these star figures strolled into the room where Ralph was sitting, suddenly startled by this seeming contact with the past. Did lord lieutenants sport a colourful uniform and a sheathed sword? So impressive.

Low Pastures had stables, a broad, part-gravelled, part-tarmacked drive, lined with beech, conifers and larch, and a view of the docks and distant sea. There were paddocks where his daughters could train up their ponies for gymkhana bouts. Ponies and a groom for them Ralph considered brought a nice touch of distinction, especially if there were spares: the children could take their pick of four at any time.

'Low Pastures has put on at least a million in the last nine or ten months,' Ralph said. 'That's not just my guess. I bumped into Miles Ross-Hilton, estate agent supreme, who says so. OK, property values have climbed pretty well everywhere in the UK, but not by anything near our rate here.'

'Bingo!' she said. 'Boom! Bonanza!'

'In a way.'

'The wrong way?' she asked.

'Could be.'

'Seems crazy to be troubled by doing well, Ralph.'

'I know. Paradox. I'm so fond of the place, can't bear to see it menaced.'

Certain quirky features at Low Pastures had always delighted Ralph and kept a gentle, encouraging grip on his affections. One of his favourites was a small blue plaque that someone – someone learned – in the far-off past had fixed to a kitchen garden gate. This Ralph cleaned thoroughly every few weeks, an enjoyable duty. It bore a Latin inscription: '*Mens cuiusque is est quisque.*' Not an x in sight.

Ralph had done some research and discovered it came from Cicero, a top-notch ancient scholar, meaning 'A man's mind is what he is.' Ralph thought Cicero seemed to be saying that a person's mind is so dominant that it takes over the rest of him – makes one quality uniquely important, like that character in a Monty Python Latin-land sketch who's known as Biggus Dickus.

Ralph had been determined to keep the message legible. He considered it brought a noble comment to the Low Pastures domain. Also it reminded him of a song sometimes performed by a group at The Monty, a club he owned: 'Is you is or is you ain't my baby?' Ralph had always been interested in questions of identity.

The blue of the plaque was very pale. Decades of weathering might help account for this. But Ralph had the notion that whoever installed the plaque would not have wanted a bolder, brasher colour, clashing with the mild, thoughtful, unshowy remark by Cicero. Although the translations always referred only to *men*'s minds, Ralph thought some women had minds, too, particularly with feminism so strong lately. That might not have been the case back in Cicero's time, B.C.

Margaret definitely had a mind, sharp and sensible, and Ralph was almost always entirely willing to discuss quite serious topics with her. If she wanted to go in for smart-arse words like 'paradox', that was absolutely OK with him. Tolerance: in a marriage you had to offer some of that now and then, even oftener.

It was late afternoon. The sun would soon drop out of sight, but for a couple of minutes it put a dark red glow on the tall, elegant, narrow windows of the house. Ralph liked narrow windows. He thought they resembled loopholes in a castle wall, ready to help repel an attack. He and Margaret were having a stroll together around the Low Pastures acreage. She had on black shorts and a yellow cotton jacket over a' white singlet.

'I think you can spot how matters might get a bit rough, for Low Pastures and the club,' he said.

'Maybe,' Margaret replied.

'It's a matter of mind, isn't it? A busy mind like yours is bound to see the—'

'Ah, Ralph, you've been browsing the garden gate again.'

'Cicero was a bright bloke,' he replied.

'You could say that.'

'He would have been pleased to know his comment got placed at a kitchen garden.'

'Yes?' Margaret said.

Ralph pointed at the gate: 'Indicates the mind is more important than the food growing there because the mind is what a man or woman is, not just somebody who eats parsnips. Perhaps he was addressing pupils and wanted them to get their priorities right: not stomach, brain.'

'When I look at the current situation I see four people,' Margaret said. 'You, of course, Ralph, then Mansel Shale, then Des Iles and his right-hand man, Detective Chief Superintendent Colin Harpur. Possibly these last two, and especially Iles, are the most crucial.' Now and then Margaret thought Ralph should be hauled in from life's larger topics and made to deal with some of the basics.

'Perhaps,' Ralph said. Yes, Margaret had a mind all right.

'Iles and his very cooperative blind eye, C. Harpur,' Margaret said.

'Iles, the policy-maker,' Ralph said.

'You could put it like that. But a policy that is a kind of non-policy,' she replied. 'Nothing happens.'

'You could put it like that. I don't think I understand what you mean when you talk of "the current situation".'

'Of course you do, Ralph.'

'No.'

'The situation of this city,' Margaret said.

'What is it?'

'Super-rich, super-vulnerable,' Margaret said.

THREE

Several days – or rather nights – after this conversation, Ralph had a couple of after-midnight visitors at The Monty, the stay-late social club he owned in Shield Terrace. He'd been expecting them. Ralph prized his ability to look ahead, especially to spot signs of, and sources of, possible trouble. He felt this was vital in someone who headed two notable businesses. Responsibility. Anticipation. He'd devised a slogan to sum up his attitude: 'The present does not guarantee the future.' Ralph was quite fond of slogans. They should be distilled wisdom. They offered ungabby, clear guidance. Ralph believed wholeheartedly in ungabbiness. There wasn't much of it about. But perhaps that was natural with ungabbiness!

As he'd hinted to Margaret, his wife, things were going too well in this city. Of course, he realized that sounded totally nuts. Too much peace? Too much contentment? Oh, for fuck's sake, come on! But, she'd called it a paradox. And he'd seen a definition of a paradox which he thought really clicked: 'Truth standing on its head to attract attention.' He believed that, on the quiet, Margaret half accepted his view of things.

It was surely true that things could be not just good but too bloody good, provocatively good, in this city – in any city. Too good because it naturally caused fierce, violent envy and prompted outsiders to come in and get a juicy slice of it, or get all of it. Predators saw signals, and were very ready to respond. Margaret was, of course, totally right when she said that Ralph had no difficulty understanding what she meant when speaking of the city's situation. He knew it very well.

And the central, essential factor in that situation was the certainty that nothing would stop the drugs business. Survival was built-in and impregnable. This wasn't just about the drugs trafficking here. General. Everywhere. The other central and essential factor was that Iles and Harpur knew this and shaped their policy in clever accordance: they accommodated, went gently and permissively, not harshly prohibitive because harshly prohibitive didn't – couldn't – work; meant suffering, bloodshed, death.

At present, Ralph reckoned the recreational substances business here went along sweetly and efficiently, like any other worthwhile commerce. That was Ralph's main earner, the club only secondary, a far-back secondary, though he had a ceaseless longing to jack up The Monty's social class, get it to rate with, say, The Athenaeum in London. The very securely established, comfortable trading was bound to seem attractive territory for other big-time pushers elsewhere, like virgin forest to an explorer. When Ralph heard of the gorgeously dressed, multi-shot, very non-local stiff found lately in dockland he had wondered at once whether it signalled the start of an onslaught; or probably more than one onslaught, and the result of vicious competition and cruel turf warfare between grab-all newcomers. 'Expand or die' was well-known business advice.

Ralph believed Assistant Chief Constable Iles would be very curious, possibly anxious. After all, he was designer and architect of the well-behaved, cosy drugs merchandising, 'blind-eye' police toleration of it – in Margaret's words – as long as there were no killings or injuries, no blood on the pavement or, on what Ralph had heard was the ducky three-piece suit, and possibly on a lot more three-piece suits: the gangs dressed nicely. Ralph had assumed Iles would look in at The Monty for a discussion of the possible new conditions, and to find whether Ralph knew any more about them. Ralph had at least as much to lose as Iles, or that's how Ralph thought the ACC would reason

Now, just before 1.30 a.m. at the club, here Iles was, his usual colleague, Detective Chief Superintendent Colin Harpur, with him, Iles in uniform, Harpur wearing what Iles would undoubtedly regard as one of his miserable, off-the-peg civvy suits, without a waistcoat and probably nowhere near the corpse's outfit for swank and brilliant lapels.

Ralph was at his little desk behind the bar checking receipts and invoices when the pair arrived. Immediately, he stood to

greet them, as if warmly: Ralph didn't want to be talked down
to while they were still standing. The assistant chief was
ungracious enough, without that. Getting a bonny smile of
professional bar owner's welcome in place, Ralph spent a full
half-minute searching for the right word to describe the look
on Iles's face. He came up eventually with two, 'benign' and
'empathic'. This scared him shitless. Christ, something must
be terribly wrong for Iles to masquerade as caring.

Ralph felt confused. He noticed some changes. Normally,
when Iles entered the club he would pause and gaze about
unlovingly at the members there, as if doing a happy, private
census of those he'd helped get jailed, though released now;
and others he'd be helping get jailed pretty soon. Not quite
running, but at a decent speed, several, and sometimes many,
members would leave immediately when Iles and Harpur
arrived, and Iles would yell a string of body-parts slurs after
them, including some he'd told Ralph he picked up on holiday
in the Caribbean, where slurs were an art-form.

Tonight, some people did hurriedly leave, not bothering to
finish their drinks or pool game, as soon as they saw Iles and
Harpur, but Iles didn't shout now and instead appeared
grievously saddened at losing their company. Pain and sorrow
flickered across his face, so Ralph felt convinced that
something hellish must be imminent or actually under way.

'Ralph!' Iles cried, in a chummy voice, 'how wonderful
this is! Col and I were idling – no other term will do for it,
isn't that so, Col? – yes, we were idling at headquarters,
nothing to interest us, when Col said, as if out of some useful
inspirational store, "Why don't we go to see Ralph? Always
he will give us a rousing, genial, wholehearted reception,
because that is his nature and he cannot be other than
charmingly amiable: a fine talent for friendship is in the
Ember blood."'

'We're always glad to see you and Mr Harpur,' even when
you lie, as now, Ralph said, though the latter part not spoken
but only thought.

'We count on it, Ralph,' Iles said, smiling a huge, comradely
smile to equal Ralph's. He rotated slowly, pointing to various
areas of the club bar-room as if delightfully surprised. 'And

all the repairs brilliantly completed after those recent infinitely regrettable barbaric ructions.'[2]

'Minor,' Ralph said.

'One would hardly know there had been such severe damage to The Monty's interior,' Iles said.

'Superficial,' Ralph replied. 'Members quick to help put things right, showed loyalty.'

'Only somebody who had actually seen the appalling mess here after the attack would be able to spot evidence of skilled mending and sprucing,' Iles said. 'Vandalism defeated. Transformation. Congratulations indeed!'

It could be like this with Iles: dim, apparently go-nowhere remarks, but often sidling into something unpleasant and hurtful. Yes, there had been breakages and staining in the bar not long ago, but was there any need to comment on it now? OK, the comment came in what seemed like sympathy, and admiration for the quality of the work. But, really, Iles was saying there had been terrible devastation at the club and that if fracas came once, fracas could come again, and again: fracas bred fracas.

Ralph mixed some drinks for them and one for himself and they went to sit at a bar table. Iles seemed to have recovered totally from his spasm of suffering at the departure of those members once they saw him. 'A therapy, Ralph,' he said.

'Excuse me, but what is, Mr Iles?' Ralph said.

'A visit to The Monty,' Iles said. 'A privilege.'

'Thank you, Mr Iles,' Ralph said.

'A club held in general esteem and deservedly so,' Iles replied.

'Thank you, Mr Iles,' Ralph said.

'We know you have justifiable pride in it and ambitions to make it all the more beloved and distinguished,' Iles said. 'This is to your sparkling credit.'

Ralph said: 'I don't see why only London clubs are considered to be of high reputation. I mean, The Athenaeum, The Carlton, White's. Our aim here is to challenge that traditional, cocky dominance.'

---

[2] See *Hitmen I Have Known*.

'Good on you, Ralph,' Iles said. 'Success to the reborn, Monty!'

Ralph, though, was watching Harpur. The detective chief super didn't take part in what Ralph regarded as the ACC's smarmy, token tribute to the club. Ralph could tell that Harpur's mission was to check security and defences. He sipped at his plebby mixed gin and cider and gazed methodically about over the rim of his glass. For quite a time he stared at the thick steel sheet hanging on lengths of chain over the spot where Ralph had his desk, the chains safely anchored in stout ceiling beams.

He reckoned that this heavy metal slab would give him decent protection if some hired gun got into the club at the main entrance and tried to destroy him with a small-arms volley. The possibility of direct, straight marksmanship, or markswomanship, from the doorway had made him feel badly exposed, and he'd decided to reduce that threat. He usually had bouncers on duty, but someone really determined and needing the fee would probably push or sneak past and do swift damage, swift damage meaning the eternal shut-down of Ralph. As could be honestly said about so many of these business ploys, no personal hate featured. They were transaction only. Nothing personal.

Although he could not think of a sweeter place to die than in his cherished Monty, best not die at all, yet. There were certainly folk about who would like him gone. And there might be more of them soon. Ralph would avoid getting obsessive and nervous about his safety, but he aimed to be as safe as could be arranged, with the help of this hi-fli, custom-made rampart. There was a danger that this thick metal slab would seem too stark, so he'd had it covered with stick-on illustrations from a work called *The Marriage of Heaven and Hell* by William Blake.

'What about this murder?' he said. Ralph wanted to switch the conversation away from what might be considered sensitive areas for him, and on to an area not very favourable for Iles. No arrests yet.

'Murder? Which?' Iles said.

'The tailor's dummy,' Ralph replied. 'An outsider. The story is, I gather, two, possibly three rounds in the head.'

'Yes, a story,' Harpur said.

'Any murder, two, three or ten bullets, we'll be working on it, be sure of that, Ralph,' Iles said. 'Outsider or local, Col will give the same thoroughness. Whatever else we might think of him, Harpur is thorough.'

'Why is this stranger here in our city?' Ralph replied.

'"Stranger? Outsider?" Oh you've been reading Camus again, have you, Ralph?' Iles said. 'His work *L'Étranger*, *The Stranger*, that title, often translated, though, as *The Outsider*. But we won't go along with his argument that the world is meaningless and all attempts to impose order absurd. We believe in order, don't we, Ralph, and we'll oppose those who try to muck it about, befoul it? Certainly, that's one of the lines Col will follow,' Iles said. 'We will always resist imported disorder and thuggery. If we must stand alone, we *will* stand alone, and steadfastly block all attempts to refashion us.'

'Are things turning vicious?' Ralph said.

'Which things?' Iles said.

'The scene,' Ralph replied. 'Trends. The general, all-round condition of things.'

'But which things?' Iles said.

'Things overall,' Ralph said.

'Col is a bit hot and cold on trends,' Iles replied.

'Because he's not consistent it doesn't mean they don't exist,' Ralph said.

'Ah, now you're getting deep,' Iles said. He chuckled forgivingly. 'What's the difference between ignorance and absence? That's a well-known metaphysical tease isn't it, much jostled with, by philosophers A.J. Ayer and the Vienna Circle? Camus one minute, Ralph, Ayer the next! You're really turning intellectual.'

Ralph thought Harpur seemed to tire of the assistant chief's performance. Maybe Harpur would like a change of topics, pronto. And perhaps he had finished his survey of the bar. He put his empty glass on the table. 'The future, Ralph. To some degree it's what might be called paradoxical.'

Iles said: 'Col gets to the roots, and at the roots he finds a paradox, Ralph, are you all right with that term?'

'Which?' Ralph said.

'Paradox,' Iles said.

'How do you mean, "all right"?' Ralph replied.

'Understand,' Iles said.

'Understand? I think of it as, oh, how can I say? . . . I think of it as truth standing on its head to attract attention,' Ralph replied. Strange to hear Iles echo Margaret – there must be something worth thinking about in 'paradox'.

'Nice,' Iles replied. 'You've got a flair for the visual.'

'Quite a lot of them about,' Ralph said.

'What?' Iles said.

'Paradoxes,' Ralph said. 'This dead man in the suit seems to have brought them.'

'In a way, yes,' Harpur replied.

'Col will get to it,' Iles said, 'despite how he looks – the haircut and so on and the garments. Regardless of all that there's a bit of a brain occasionally quite active. If this deceased can set off the paradoxes, Col will probably spot it,' Iles said. 'I've seen him deal with more than one tricky challenge. Yes, I'm fairly sure it's more than one.'

Harpur decided it was time for him to chip in: 'We know, don't we, that outsider business leaders see our area as an extremely attractive spread because, thanks very much to Mr Iles, and in part to you, Ralph and Mansel Shale, it is a tranquil, serene sort of haven, the trading well-regulated, untroublesome and untroubled, and therefore always profitable, not just for the commodities business, but the business scene altogether, because of the calm, settled atmosphere.'

'It's a living,' Ralph said.

'Our peacefulness here is very much the crux,' Harpur said.

'Show Harpur a crux and he'll move in on it. He'll see offshoots,' Iles replied.

'Some of these would-be incomers want this peace so that they can sell their stuff unbothered, unbuggered about, and they are most likely ready to fight, maim and kill for such conditions if they have to,' Harpur said. This, Harpur more or less believed.

'Ah,' Iles said, doing an ecstatic imitation hands-clap, 'we're here.'

'Where?' Ralph said.

'We've reached the paradox: they want peace but will battle to get it, if they must,' Iles replied. 'Heard of someone called Chail? Of course you have.'

'They would destroy what they're fighting for,' Harpur said. 'And, of course, they see the huge, arrant stupidity of this. They're not dim. These are business people who've built successful firms against the competition. They want a future. They're constructive. They've got enough to worry about already with the rumours that the world will stop using cash in favour of cards or bank transfers. How do you run a drugs company if you can't use cash – every other form of money is very traceable? They would like to avoid warfare if it can be avoided. After all, it's the present absence of warfare that attracts and drives them. They've seen the stats showing a steep rise in coke use by households with incomes above £50k a year. They'll assume the growth must be especially rosy on our patch because wealthy families will want to come and settle here for the comfortable conditions and easy substance availability They can afford our madly high property prices, booming from demand and scarcity.'

'Solutions?' Iles said. But Ralph knew the assistant chief was not asking a question. The flutey lilt had gone out of his voice. He would *name* the solutions, not listen to them. 'They will come to talk to you, Ralph, and to Manse Shale.'

'Who will?' Ralph said.

'Kingpins from other firms – intruders or would-be intruders,' Iles said.

'Wasting their time,' Ralph said.

'They'll be lining up to talk to you and to Manse,' Iles said. 'And what they'll propose is a sort of alliance, a sort of merger, with you and Mansel Shale.'

'Ridiculous,' Ralph said.

'On the face of it, yes,' Iles replied. 'Why should you and/ or Manse respond to that kind of offer – those kinds of offers, because there will be several, no question?'

'Yes, why?' Ralph said.

Harpur said: 'They would like "an arrangement" with successful existing firms, and if that can't be achieved, they'll take the obvious next option, that is, wipe out the inconvenient existing firms – yours, Manse's. Violence, ruthlessness. And even if they got an agreement to operate here, they'd probably tire of it pretty soon and turn to that same violence and ruthlessness and get rid of you or Manse, anyway. By then they'd possibly have new incursors to preoccupy themselves with and handle.'

'We've already discussed bits of this situation, Ralph, haven't we?' Iles said. 'You'll get a gushing spiel about cooperation – increased scale and therefore sales. You'll hear a sermon about the security of size. Bernard Chail, or someone like him, will describe for you the magnificent strengths of a cartel, or even a monopoly. And, above all, of course, they'll glorify what used to be called by fingers-crossed international politicians last century, "peaceful co-existence."'

'Manse Shale and I already have that,' Ralph said. 'We divide the ground. The border lines are clear and respected, any disputes quickly resolved.'

'That's why other traders envy you,' Iles said, 'and why they want to get incorporated as your associates, now, but with a view to taking the lot pretty soon. It's classic infiltration. Col wants you to grasp this, Ralph. He believes that's where the direst peril lies. And on this kind of thing – peril and direness – he's not always totally wrong.'

'Maybe our dead visitor in the memorable garb came here seeking possible openings for one of the scheming parties and was seen off by somebody from the opposition,' Harpur said.

'Defence,' Iles said, in a very caring tone. 'We'd like to feel you have strong defences.'

'Yes?' Ralph said.

'Col worries about your lack of protection,' Iles said. 'Col *is* a worrier. Fret badgers him. This has its positive side. He looks at the pictures and is hit hard by anxiety, and who am I to say it's not warranted?'

'Pictures? Which pictures?' Ralph said.

'Very graphic,' Iles replied. 'Terrifyingly graphic.'

'Graphic of what?' Ralph said.

'Location,' Harpur said. 'Landscape. We've got aerials.'

'Aerials?' Ralph said.

'Overhead photographs,' Iles said.

'Overhead?' Ralph replied.

'Taken from a plane or helicopter,' Harpur said.

'Oh,' Ralph said.

'It's routine,' Iles said.

'What is?' Ralph said.

'Pics of substantial properties, liable to get targeted,' Iles said. 'I'd regard Low Pastures as substantial, wouldn't you, Ralph?'

'Targeted?' Ralph replied.

'You've taken very beguiling and wise precautions here in the club,' Iles said. He nodded towards the floating, bulletproof *Marriage of Heaven and Hell*. 'Ideal. But it's your home, Low Pastures, that bothers Harpur. We see on the photos so much easily crossed space around the building – paddocks, lawns, a putting green, kitchen garden. True, there's a gate, but not the sort of gate that would keep anyone out. It has what seems to be a plaque on it with an inscription, but unreadable at this distance.

'The drive is lined with trees and bushes offering plentiful cover for anyone making a stealth-type approach. Low Pastures and its park were conceived as a gentleman's residence, not a kind of fortress designed to stop murder teams. And so Harpur's unease.' Rumours had reached Ralph that Iles was seriously looking for a full chief post elsewhere. Was his worried tone only a show?

'When Mr Iles says "targeted", he's thinking of what could happen at next stage if the merger talks break down, Ralph.'

'As they almost certainly will,' Iles said. 'We don't expect any enthusiasm from you or Mansel for some merger proposal. Things could turn rough, then.'

'Well, they have begun to turn rough already, haven't they? We have a dead man. But we mean rough for you, Ralph, rough for Manse,' Harpur said.

Ralph felt bombarded from two sides, and would bet it was just what this sly pair had planned. He didn't altogether understand why they were here or what they wanted, but they obviously – or not so obviously – wanted something. Ralph reckoned he had to cope not with that famous hard-cop, soft-cop trick, but slippery cop, more-slippery cop. They took over automatically from each other in the misty chatter, as if the message was so powerful and crucial it couldn't be analysed solo, only in relays.

'And the photos show some considerable building work under way at one end of the house, giving more cover behind heavy machinery and possibly extra, unusual entry points to the property,' Iles said.

'Extension of the east wing,' Ralph said. 'Modest. I need a gallery for some art, and collections of china and porcelain in showcases.'

'Of course you do,' Iles replied. 'This is normal for someone of your status and income. But Harpur would most likely regard it as a provocation to your business rivals.'

'Regard what as a provocation?' Ralph said.

'Someone, already the proud owner of a large, classy mansion, now wants to make it even larger so it can house pricey exhibits. Am I right and you'd regard it as a provocation, Col?' Iles said.

'People take different views on a range of topics,' Harpur replied.

'Deep,' Iles said. 'Harpur can be very deep, Ralph. I know nobody comfier with clichés than Col.'

'Provocation how?' Ralph replied.

'Art. China,' Iles said.

'What about them?' Ralph said.

'People out there might have heard of the art and the china and porcelain displays. And what does it say to them, Ralph?' Iles asked.

'Say to them?' Ralph replied.

'Their reaction, their opinions,' Iles said. 'These items speak in their quiet but emphatic style of a certain way of life, don't they, of a certain standard of life, not commonplace or measly.'

'Which items?' Ralph said.

'Nice paintings, fine china saucers, historic wassail bowls,' Iles said.

'Beautiful things need to be properly installed – that's what I feel,' Ralph said. 'It's simple logic and follow-through. I see it as an act of respect towards the articles concerned, especially if there's a historic aspect.'

'Beautiful, expensive things,' Iles said. 'Rare things out of most people's reach.'

'Rarity often means cost,' Ralph said. 'First rule of the market. Think of that Victorian Penny Black postage stamp.'

'And you can afford that cost,' Iles replied, 'plus the builder's bill for a bigger east wing.'

'Nothing very grand,' Ralph said.

'A wing,' Iles said. 'Wings and wassail bowls, Ralph, excite interest, even wings deemed modest by their owner. There are folk running apparently profitable firms elsewhere who haven't got house wings, big or less big, or wassail bowls.

'This gives rise to that rather vile quality I've already mentioned – envy, a deadly sin, Ralph, and one that can provoke any afflicted by it into violent, destructive, possibly lethal attack, I fear. For them, Ralph Ember's domain comes to look like the promised land, flowing with easy money. They'll try to make the promise get real, possibly using that kind of brutal, destructive, lethal attack if gentlemanly negotiations fail, and the extreme likelihood is that they will.'

Ralph watched Iles shake his head slowly three times as though signalling massively painful regret at this prospect. The ACC took a large sip, bordering on a gulp, of what he always referred to as his 'old tarts' drink', a port and lemon. This seemed to strengthen him and bring on further insights. Ralph still didn't get his and Harpur's purpose, though.

'And then we must note the nature of the things to be kept in the extra wing,' Iles said. 'What do we make of that, the art, the chic crockery? They are, aren't they, possessions arranged for contemplation? They will be gazed at admiringly, the circumstances sedate, reverential, wholly unraucous. In other words, Ralph, they mirror and symbolize the kind of conditions that prevail generally in our city – the kind of conditions that will attract those who hunger for serenity, safe relaxation, happy homeliness. That lovely, fragile china can sit there secure and utterly unshattered behind glass because their owner believes in well-managed, restrained living, maybe helped along a little by bracing, very positive sale of the commodities every day and night to our grateful customers. I expect you've read Stephen Pinker's book, *The*

Better Angels of Our Nature, about the decline of violence in these times.'

'I might have missed that,' Ralph replied.

'Published in 2010 or thereabouts,' Iles said. 'It would help to explain why people come here to escape from violence. We are fashionable. We are brilliant, inspiring examples. Of course, the theory doesn't always stand up long-term. Greedy crooks will take to violence again if things don't work out suitably for them. This is paradox country again.

'The trouble, as they see it, is that this owner – Ralph W. Ember – doesn't want to give up any fraction of his influence and earnings from this healthy system and so might have to be slaughtered, along with his mate, Manse. Excuse me, Ralph, but what follows is delicate. Your wife and children, snug as they think – snug and secure in Low Pastures – would prob-ably be entirely unaware of the threat, and of possibly being . . . here comes that unpleasant but necessary word again, Ralph . . . not aware of being perhaps targeted,' Iles said, 'targeted simply because they're yours.'

At about that point, Ralph began to understand why these two might be here. It enraged him again. He could tell once more that those disgusting hints from his past lived and flour-ished in their lazy, slipshod minds. They had fastened on to those foul reports that blamed him for cowardice of some sort, an age ago maybe putting pals in peril, maybe even causing pals' deaths. When they saw or thought about him it wasn't simply as he was now, but as he was rumoured to have been at some incident or incidents years ago. Fear: they seemed to believe he was permanently and hopelessly governed by fear. They *wanted* to believe it. They'd decided fear ran him, how a jockey ran a horse. They almost certainly reckoned that if faced by a merger proposal, he would kowtow to its terms, terrified not to, terror being his usual, inherited condition. Bring out the fucking white flag from where it was kept freshly laundered.

Ralph had heard of a quality called the 'ruling passion'. It referred to someone's main personal quality – the one that explained all the rest of him or her. Fright: did Iles regard that as Ralph's ruling passion? This question suddenly tore into him and made Ralph realize why Harpur and Iles visited tonight.

Ralph felt they'd try to convince him that, even if he did cave in to a poisonous offer, it would only postpone the savagery. Ralph remembered an Iles phrase: 'classic infiltration', classic meaning bags of previous cases. It was infiltration as a start only, as a beginning only. The newcomers would soon go for full possession, not a sweetly dignified, share-and-share-alike partnership. And they'd crush any opposition and take what they fancied. This included the precious art, china and porcelain in the expanded east wing; and possibly not just the contents of that charmingly improved bit of property, but the bit of property itself, and even the whole Low Pastures package, building and terrain. It would be used to getting taken over by powerful people, such as a Spanish consul and a lord lieutenant in history.

All this added up to one blunt message from Iles and Harpur, and, of course, it was a message that Ralph found entirely right and good. He could purr agreement with this message. Certainly he could. If he was into composing messages himself, this might be the kind he'd send.

But, although he agreed absolutely with what the message said, it angered him that they clearly felt compelled to deliver it urgently to him, as though otherwise he might go under, might crumple, might fall apart before he could be given some guts. Was this a respectful way to deal with Ralph W. Ember of Low Pastures and The Monty? Was it, fuck! In their devious, contemptible fashion, they insisted there could be no effective change from the present smooth arrangement between Ralph and the ACC – peace in our time its admirable, wholesome aim. Although this was not a particularly usual arrangement – top cop, drugs commodore – it worked. Until now, that is; and Ralph thought it beautifully comfortable. But for them to behave as though he lacked the will and courage to help guard this fine, time-blessed set-up was surely a rotten smear.

Ralph realized his own interests were not the only ones involved. Obviously ACC Iles wouldn't want on his ground a bigger recreational business, headed by unpredictable, potentially very aggressive strangers. And it would be even bigger if

Mansel Shale's handsome empire also was infiltrated and colonized.

'I'm going to increase patrols around Low Pastures and on the route from there to the club and back, Ralph,' Iles said. 'Oh, I'm sure you'll protest and say it's not necessary and meddlesome. But you're regularly driving there alone late at night. And we'll keep an eye on your children – gymkhanas, netball, school, that kind of scene. We're devoted to holy status-quo-dom, aren't we, Col?'

Harpur didn't answer.

'Yes, I do feel none – none of this might be necessary,' Ralph said.

'None of which, Ralph?' Iles said.

'We're talking about possibilities, not facts,' Ralph replied.

'Thank you for the correction, I'm sure,' Iles said.

'Anyone could have made this point,' Ralph said.

'Yes, anyone could have,' Iles said. 'Dozy, bland unpreparedness is commonplace. I'll increase the patrols, I think. We don't want you riddled and leaking Kressmann's Armagnac on to the highway, Ralph. That's your tipple, isn't it?'

FOUR

Abbout a week later, at 2.15 a.m., driving up alone towards Low Pastures, near Apsley Farm, Harpur saw a parked Volvo in a layby ahead, no lights. It was a fine, almost cloudless night. As he drew nearer, he could make out two people in the front seats, the one behind the wheel possibly a woman. Good: he was half-expecting to see a parked, occupied car showing no lights on this stretch of road now. As for stretches of road, this stretch could be notable and he needed to be on it and taking a look.

Although the two in the Volvo wore plain clothes, Harpur knew they must be one of the ACC's increased patrols. He'd mentioned the route Ralph Ember generally took to get back to Low Pastures after a late-night spell at The Monty.

Harpur had decided to do a couple of checks and make sure the new 'arrangements' were functioning OK. It suited him anyway to come out tonight. Denise, his undergraduate girlfriend, had gone home to Stafford for her mother's birthday and wasn't sleeping at Harpur's house in Arthur Street as she often did – some nights there, some in her room at Jonson Court, a student accommodation block without an h. It was easier to leave his bed when Denise wasn't in it. Harpur's daughters also liked it when she stopped over and cooked special breakfasts, heavy on the black pudding.

Harpur didn't mind all that much giving up a couple of hours for a little non-urgent tour. He assumed it would be non-urgent, though Iles had astonishingly sharp instincts and frequently spotted big trouble on the way before anyone else noticed, Harpur sometimes included.

He pulled in and parked partway along the Volvo so he and the driver could talk with their side windows rolled down. He recognized Detective Sergeant Tracy Dilk now. In the passenger seat alongside her was Detective Constable Roy

Verity-Wright. 'Good morning, Mr Harpur,' Tracy said. 'We've nothing to report.'

Tracy was cheerful, quick to cotton on, her fair hair cut short, snub nosed, small chinned, tipped for fast promotion. 'Nothing moves, total stillness,' she said. 'Explainable: our unit watching The Monty tell us he's going to be later than usual. There's a big club thrash celebrating Intelligent Percy's acquittal against the odds in that wounding with intent trial verdict yesterday.'

'We've been discussing this lurking roadside duty, Mr Harpur,' Roy said, speaking across Tracy.

'Well, I suppose so,' Harpur replied. Roy was new to the Force and Harpur guessed he'd be striving to get the tone of things. Harpur could imagine what a tough exercise this must be for someone unfamiliar with police methods here. Roy was about twenty-six, lean, long faced, athletic looking, smooth voiced.

'Out on a quiet country road at this time of night,' Roy said. 'Why is Ralphy Ember so precious?'

'He doesn't like being called Ralphy. It's Ralph or Ember,' Harpur said.

'But why so precious to Mr Iles? He's behind this operation, isn't he?' Roy said.

'He's assistant chief (Operations),' Harpur said. He would frequently hear this kind of niggly inquiry about Iles. Even more frequently, he'd be aware of it hovering near during a conversation, though not actually spoken, perhaps from tact, more likely from uneasiness. These questions asked in their various forms, and behind their suggestive, evasive, money-bags words like 'precious', whether Iles was on Ember's payroll, and obliged to look after him in case Ralph and the stipend were abruptly stopped.

Harpur knew that Iles would never touch that kind of relationship, or that kind of money – would regard both as ridiculously beneath him – but Harpur also knew how it must appear to someone like Roy, fresh to the situation, unfledged, and with his own rather inaccurate idea of how policing functioned, possibly, and more than possibly, familiar with TV documentaries or playlets about police corruption where officers were bought by criminals for their influence.

'Mr Iles is to do with operations but also with overall policy,' Tracy said.

Harpur was thankful for her intervention. It didn't really say much – perhaps she genuinely didn't believe Iles bribable just as Harpur didn't – or not much that actually answered Roy's queries—but she saved Harpur from having to say something empty and trite himself.

'It's a matter of domain, is it?' Roy said. He gave that word, 'domain', a hearty emphasis.

'Domain?' Harpur replied. He tried to call up in his memory Roy's CV. Did he have a degree in history, perhaps *ancient* history?

'Realm,' Roy said. 'His territory. Do you know whom it reminds me of when people speak of Mr Iles, sir?'

'Who's that then, Roy?' Harpur said, getting some strong interest into his tone.

'King Ashurdanipal of Assyria.'

'Ah, yes, of course,' Harpur said.

'Shouldn't that be Ashurbanipal?' Tracy said.

'There's the famous excavated stone relief known as *The Lion Hunt*,' Roy said. 'It shows the king fighting off the savage beasts because as monarch he has a duty to create and preserve order, and the lions represent an evil threat from outside.

'Is Mr Iles in that role? We are deputed on the assistant chief's behalf to repel a threat, but we don't know where it's supposed to be coming from or even what or who it is,' Roy said.

'Not lions,' Harpur replied. Sometimes he wondered whether recruiting graduates at all was very wise.

'I don't think we've been briefed in detail on our function here,' Roy said. 'Very non-specific. We are like traffic cops but are not traffic cops.'

'The worst threats are often like that,' Tracy said. 'Undefined, at least early on.'

'Right,' Harpur said.

'Something else troubles me,' Roy said.

'Oh, yes?' Harpur replied.

'Sergeant Dilk is armed, but not me,' Roy said.

'You're still due a gun course,' Tracy said.

'Does Mr Iles think Ralph Ember is essential to good order and lawfulness on his bailiwick?' Roy replied. 'Doesn't he think his officers are capable of doing the job?'

'Mr Iles is a real fan of peace,' Harpur said.

'And he thinks that a drugs tycoon will help him secure it?' Roy replied. 'Or two drugs tycoons, if we take in Mansel Shale's companies?'

'Manse is certainly part of the general scene,' Harpur said, 'and part of a happy collab with Ember.'

'So I've heard,' Roy said.

'Oh, yes. That's a remarkable, enduring, tranquil dual-act, Ralph and Manse,' Harpur said.

'And cheered on by Mr Iles?' Roy asked. He sounded amazed, horrified now.

'Peace is a slippery item, Roy,' Harpur said. 'Not everyone is in the hunt for it, and so there'll be strange alliances, unspoken bargains, stretched tolerance.'

'Yes, but—'

'In London peace has gone absent. Murders daily. Gang-based,' Harpur said. 'Mr Iles hates that sort of degenerate turmoil, doesn't want such appalling break-down here – thinks it unnecessary and his mission is to prevent it. Maybe it can develop in Manchester, possibly Birmingham, but it's not us. And it won't be us for as long as Mr Iles is in charge.'

'Unnecessary?' Roy replied. 'A strange word in this context, if I may say so, sir. Obviously, it couldn't be thought of as necessary.'

'Exactly.' Harpur started his engine.

'The question has to be, "Is he actually in charge?",' Roy said.

'I'll take a swift look at Low Pastures,' Harpur replied. He drew away from the Volvo.

FIVE

Harpur didn't know much about age-old houses, but he did know that some people were very keen on properties with a lot of history, preferably standing alone in their own grounds, though a lengthy past was the absolute essential, not the location. Low Pastures could claim both: Harpur had heard it dated from the seventeenth century, and the house stood solo, surrounded by its lawns, gardens, walks, pergolas, paddocks, a small arboretum, stables, patios. It was approached by a broad tree-and-bush-lined drive, part gravelled, part tarmac.

Distinguished people had occupied this estate at various periods over the centuries. Harpur knew Ralph Ember was exceptionally pleased and proud to figure in that succession, and aimed to be absolutely worthy of it – a compulsion. He could reason, couldn't he, that if impressive figures had lived here in the past, then its owner now must inherit a fair portion of that impressiveness? Well, no, that wasn't in the least logical. It didn't at all follow that personal distinction came with the title-deeds. But Ralph could probably kid himself that it did. He would most likely feel able to shut out from this inane but comforting deduction the fact that, not long before Ralph moved in, Low Pastures had been occupied by an outright, brutal villain, Caring Oliver Leach. Did he inherit some of this impressiveness, too? Not that Harpur had heard. He understood, though, why Low Pastures did so much for Ralph's morale and ego.

It was a couple of miles from the Volvo layby to Low Pastures. As he drove, Harpur went over in his memory bits of the conversation with Verity-Wright and Tracy. He thought Roy might be OK despite that cumbersome, showy education. Some questions were best kept shelved.

No, Roy couldn't have the replies he wanted and almost forgivably felt entitled to, but Harpur thought Roy did get something to consider while he and Tracy waited for Ralph, and whatever else – 'and whatever else' being why they were there. Harpur wondered if Roy might begin to realize as he took on his new job that it was like entering a country of bewilderingly vague outlines and borders, some considerable areas extremely murky and misleading or blocked off; but very small sectors of it nearly clear-cut and untricky.

Ember would probably have been able to explain some of these deep complications to Roy. Harpur felt sure Ralph was stuck with an awkward load of them. For instance, think of The Monty and Intelligent Percy's non-clink gala there tonight. Ralph, this ardent, indomitable seeker after respectable eminence and honour, dedicated environmentalist and enemy of river pollution, proprietor of an esteemed, time-graced, classic home, was, regardless of all that flagrant top-notchery, taking part in and hosting a grand, hearty, celebratory piss-up at the club for an infinitely dubious character, Percival Cranfield Nain, or Intelligent Percy, as he was dubbed.

OK, he had been found not guilty, and in some senses he and his shindig were totally pure, completely wholesome and innocent. But Harpur knew that in Percy's wounding case, as in so many other cases these days, it had been impossible to find witnesses brave enough to go into the box and say what they had seen. Yes, yes, it was an acquittal for lack of evidence, but what brand of acquittal? Would Verity-Wright be able to get his head around this? Roy might need another year or two in the job for such brands of setback to seem normal. Roy would come to realize why so many cases brought by the police depended on informants. Although informants did not appear at trials, because they could give detectives only tip-offs, not proper evidence, the tip-offs could be priceless. Perhaps that was the wrong word: most informants were paid.

Harpur thought Ralph might ask himself this – the validity of the acquittal – though probably not out loud, and definitely not out loud if Intelligent was close by. Percy had been declared guiltless, but he did know about knives. Ralph himself could still get caught up in a dire hotchpotch of possible reactions. First, he'd fear that news of his loud,

comradely involvement in Percy's sleazy carnival at The
Monty would spread. This must disastrously damage Ralph's
holy, preposterous crusade to improve the club's profile and
lift it into the same class as, say, The Athenaeum in London.
Ralph might be willing to admit that The Athenaeum could
have a member nicknamed Intelligent, but it would be for
winning the Nobel prize, not for repeatedly making the police
and courts look twats.

Secondly, though, while Ralph would certainly realize how
risky it was to encourage and cheer on tonight's crummy
jubilation, he had to oblige because The Monty was his, and
The Monty had – in Ralph's unwavering opinion – a famous,
positive, warm, major social role in this city, and might
soon become even more major when he started a series of
improvements.

Ralph would be accustomed to such confusion, such a
frustrating jumble, such contradictions. His middle name
could have been Contradictions, but in fact it was Wyverne.
If he and Roy met and had a little time, Ralph could certainly
tell him about the troublesome shifts and staggering variety
hereabouts. Stay alert, Roy!

Harpur passed the entrance to Low Pastures' drive and
parked on a patch of grass a little way beyond. He took a
torch from his car and walked back. He tried to step quietly.
He wanted to have a quick, private look at the house close to,
and particularly at the extension works mentioned by Iles.
The ACC was probably right to sense extra danger. As much
as possible, Harpur would imagine and imitate the possible
approach of someone – perhaps more than one – aiming to
get at Ralph and/or his family. It might help Harpur plan Low
Pastures' defences.

The fact that Ralph wasn't here now didn't matter very
much. It was the vulnerability or not of the house that
concerned Harpur. It concerned him because it had obviously
concerned Iles, and Iles didn't get concerned easily, except
about his Adam's apple.

Harpur realized that when Ralph saw the Volvo on his
journey home, he would tense up and wonder why they were
there. This wasn't a much-used bit of road. What orders had

those two been given? They might be in place simply to see Ralph got back to Low Pastures safely, and wouldn't need to intercept unless someone else, or, again, more than one, tried to waylay him. Harpur hoped everything would pass peacefully, and he'd gone that small distance out of sight beyond the entrance so his car wouldn't tell Ralph he had a prowler. He might be able to slip away eventually without Ralph knowing he'd been here.

Harpur didn't stay long on the Low Pastures drive. He felt obvious there. He'd be caught in Ralph's headlights if he returned shortly from the club. Harpur made his way instead across one of the paddocks towards the eastern end of the house. Scaffolding had been erected there. A JCB, a couple of wheelbarrows and a cement mixer stood nearby, and there were several metal ladders on the ground. Except for a single light over the porch, the house was dark. Harpur thought he remembered from the earlier survey that there was an anti-burglar camera over the door.

Near the edge of this paddock he saw a summerhouse, tongue-and-groove-wood-built, painted dark green to merge with the natural setting. It faced west and would get afternoon sun. Harpur liked to think of Ralph sitting on a padded garden chair in front of the summerhouse, possibly with a glass of Armagnac, planning that glorious future for The Monty. He might be making a list in his head of well-known intellectuals, business leaders and high-grade politicians – all definitely vetted by research as proven non-paederasts – who would be invited to give talks there, mentioned in advance on the public appointments page of *The Times* in the next column to the Court Circular. Ralph took *The Times* because it contained that kind of stuff. A paper like *The Sun* wouldn't have it. All *The Sun* was interested in was what celebrities, as it called them, were up to, mostly sexual.

The summerhouse had windows on both sides, and front and back, and Harpur thought it could act as an excellent security post if Iles decided Low Pastures needed serious protection, perhaps armed protection. Harpur knew that during the Irish troubles, people considered at risk often had all-weather shacks installed in their back gardens to billet minders.

The summerhouse had good vision over large stretches of the grounds, though only in front of the main house, not the rear. That area needed something different, something just as effective. To neglect the back of the property would be utterly stupid.

As far as Harpur could make out at this stage and in the dark, the addition to the building would be a two-storey job of stone about 30 feet square, pitch roofed and gabled to match the style of the main house. Some of that sand from the wharf might be in use. Harpur saw why Iles thought the work could possibly bring extra safeguarding problems. The alterations required a break through the end wall at ground and first-floor level to join the two parts of the house. Although these gaps had been boarded over and the planks nailed in place temporarily when work finished for the day, there were obvious weaknesses, almost invitations.

Harpur tried the ground-floor boards and found them absolutely firm, but the nailing could be levered out very simply with a bit of help from a jemmy when work resumed – or when a killer, killers, wanted access at a remote part of the house, less likely to be heard than a door forced or a window smashed. Harpur knew about jemmies.

He lifted one of the ladders from where they'd been piled alongside the JCB, set it against the end wall and extended it to the first floor. At his rank, should he be doing this? He thought probably not. Never mind, he'd keep it brief. He climbed quickly and tested the boards there, too. They were equally well fixed, and equally ornamental. Ember was so keen on his china, and on displaying his china in worthwhile, custom-made surroundings, that he would accept this kind of crazy risk. Well, that was Ralph, obsessed as ever by his doomed search for status and prestige. Low Pastures and its planned improvements no doubt brought high hopes. His focus on that never dimmed.

As Harpur finished his examination of the boarding and got ready to go down, thankful that his daring had turned out OK, he heard a triple rapping sound, metal on metal, from below, and there was a kind of quiver, a kind of small trembling, in the ladder's left handrail that he'd taken hold of again for the move down. He froze, tried to quieten his breathing. What had happened?

Oh, God, he mustn't fall here, perhaps disabling and/or stunning himself, so he'd be found lying there, close to the cement mixer and the ladder he was on, when the builders arrived in a few hours. If he wasn't dead, they'd call an ambulance, perhaps try the kiss-of-life and chest pummelling. Hell, what would Iles make of this when he heard? 'Fell off a ladder?' he'd say. 'Who let him near ladders? If Harpur climbed a ladder, of course he'd fall off it. Let's hope it's a head injury only – the part of him that didn't work, even before this. At Low Pastures? Was he thieving roof lead? Had a torch with him? To select the best pieces? Or was he after valuable china? There'll be breakages.'

From below a woman scream-yelled, 'Why are you here? What are you doing? Come down, sod. Who are you? Yes, come down, but, mind, I have a gun. I'll be pointing it all the way. Are you alone? How many of you? Ralph has been expecting an invasion. Are you it?' Harpur's back was towards her for the descent, and he realized that in the darkness she would not recognize him. He'd guessed at once who it must be, and he thought he knew the voice, anyway – Ember's wife, Margaret.

He half turned his head. She was in a nightdress at the foot of the ladder and wearing a Royal Enclosure brown bowler hat, too big for her and resting on her ears so they were bent double. He could just about see that she was aiming an automatic pistol at him in a proper two-handed, stiff-armed grip. She must have knocked it on the ladder to get attention before taking her gun stance, and so the banging sounds and the strange shiver in the handrail. She could have learned the approved way to direct a pistol from TV cop dramas. Probably, had heard something when in bed and come out from the front door and walked half the length of the house on patio slabs to the east wing. She had nothing on her feet.

'Harpur. Police,' he said. 'Nothing to worry you, believe me. Oh dear, have I disturbed you? Sorry.' He tried to make it a zippy conversational tone, which he thought the most reassuring and suitable for this type of ladder-dominated situation.

'Harpur?' she said. Although the tone made it a question, he thought it was not a question that showed she didn't know who Harpur was, but a question that suggested she knew who he was but did not understand why he was up a ladder at Low Pastures so late. Harpur considered that quite reasonable. He must deal with it.

He said: 'We've met once or twice, haven't we, Mrs Ember, when I've been enjoying a chat with your hubbie, Ralph, though neither of us up a ladder then?'

'Harpur? What's it about, for God's sake?'

'Complicated,' Harpur said.

'This is all outside my orbit.'

'Excuse me, but what's what about?' he said.

'This,' she said.

'Which?'

'You. The ladder. The time of night. You on our property.'

'Routine,' Harpur replied. 'It's all very much in order up here. I've done an inspection. A formality. You don't need the weapon. Not in the least. Please lower it carefully to your side, pointing at the ground. Finger off the trigger. I'm coming down.'

'Routine?' she said. 'How the fuck can it be routine, up a ladder at my house near daybreak?'

'Normal checks,' he said. 'They're recurrent in the diary. They have to be dealt with.'

'Checks of what? Why?'

'All right if I come down now?' Harpur replied.

'Will there be trouble?' she said.

'Trouble? What trouble?'

'For me,' she replied.

'Why?'

'About the gun,' she said.

'What about it?' Harpur said.

'Possession of, no licence in my name. Against the law?'

'Is it real?' Harpur said.

'Real?'

'Not an imitation? There are very good imitations.'

'It's real.'

'Loaded?'

'It feels heavy.'

'I'll come down now.' His legs were beginning to ache. 'I've finished up here. All very satis.'

'Finished what?' she said.

'The checks I mentioned.'

'But of what? No, you didn't mention—not what they were.'

'Basic.'

'The boarding?'

'There *is* boarding,' he said.

'Overnight only.'

'I'd have guessed that.'

'Why couldn't the boarding be checked in the morning or afternoon?' she replied.

'It wouldn't be there in the morning or afternoon. As you said, it's temporary. It's an attempt at security, not perfect, but the best possible.'

'Who ordered these checks? Ralph hasn't asked for them or he'd have told me,' she said. 'He's on edge a lot these days. I can tell that, but this doesn't involve the boards.'

'It's all very quick,' Harpur said.

'Ralph's not here,' she replied.

'No, I know,' Harpur said. 'He's been delayed.'

'*How* do you know?'

'I'll come down,' Harpur replied.

'It's not licensed to Ralph either, I'm pretty sure,' she said.

'The pistol is Ralph's?'

'He's secretive about guns. But I knew where this one was.'

'Looks like a Luger.' He began to descend.

'You say it was quick,' she replied.

'Well, yes.'

'But what if there hadn't been any ladders available?'

'A fair question. But there were. And there's the scaffolding.'

'Listen, Harpur, he only had the gun to protect us. Perhaps I shouldn't have intervened – disclosed too much. Ralph – you know him – he looks a bit like the young Charlton Heston. Well, youngish Charlton Heston. Heston was very keen on guns. There was more to him than El Cid in a movie. That influences Ralph. He believes he should be faithful to the memory of Chuck Heston. There's a sense of brotherliness.'

'It will probably be all right.'

'He's anxious.'

'Stress.'

'As if life's too good and is bound to turn rotten. Hubris.'

'I gather there's a lot of that about,' Harpur said.

'What?'

'Hubris.'

'Originally Greek.'

'That kind of area.'

'Do you know what it means?' she replied.

'It can strike anywhere.'

'As if to punish pride.'

'Sometimes life's OK,' Harpur said. 'Ralph has set things up pretty well for the family.'

'And you?'

'What?'

'Anxious. Why are you here, otherwise?'

'The job. A formality.'

'No car for the approach. Silent. Sneaky. But I heard you place the ladder. It woke me up. The bowler is to guard my head. I grabbed it as I came out. Ralph keeps it on a shelf in the bedroom.'

'It would be the right kind of clobber for someone living in such a property when attending a ceremonial occasion, or a horse race meeting. He likes things done correctly,' Harpur said. He reached the ground. She'd lowered the gun as he suggested. He put out his hand for it but she ignored that. The nightdress was flower patterned and had short sleeves. She was untattooed. 'Luckily, it's quite a mild night,' he said.

'Did Iles send you?' she replied.

'Mr Iles is Operations. This wouldn't rate as an operation.'

'What *would* it rate as? Could you give me a for-instance?'

'Mr Iles tries to think ahead. At his rank, that's what he has to do. It's required. He worries.'

'Is this ahead?' she replied. She gestured at where they were standing.

'Your feet,' Harpur said. 'Are they all right on this stone?
There are jagged bits.'

A vehicle moved up the drive. They watched Ember park
near the house. The porch light showed him half leave the
car but pause for a moment, as though hit by second thoughts,
his legs out of the Mercedes, the rest of him still in the
driver's seat.

'I left the front door open,' Margaret said. 'I didn't have keys
with me. He's seen it's not shut. He's bound to be shocked.'

Ralph gazed about. It would be too dark for him to see his
wife, Harpur and the ladder. He stood properly now then stepped
to the rear of the car, opened the boot and, after seeming to
rummage for a while, brought out a large, shifting spanner.
He closed the boot very gently so as to avoid noise, and the
driver's door. He had the spanner in his right hand and walked
slowly and gingerly towards the porch, swivelling now and then
to look right and left in case of intruders.

'Spanner as cosh,' Margaret said. 'You see, he doesn't carry
any of his firearms. Improvise.'

Ralph paused in the porch then went into the house. One
after the other lights came on behind uncurtained downstairs
windows. 'He's looking for me,' Margaret said.

'We should let him see you're all right,' Harpur said. 'End
his anxiety.'

'Not yet. This is good for Ralph.'

'Good for him?' Harpur said.

'A kind of treatment. It's positive.'

'In what way positive?'

'Oh, yes, therapy.'

'How?'

'Some call him Panicking Ralph, or Panicking Ralphy,
don't they – call him that behind his back? But he knows
about it. Of course he does. He's sharp. He's in touch.'

'So?' Harpur replied.

'Ralph's gone into the unknown with only a spanner. Front
door agape despite the time. This is bound to indicate peril.
Who's inside? How many? How does he protect his family
from these troublesome guests, perhaps?

'He had a very quick think and decided that, because he's without a gun, he'd better find something else. The spanner is not ideal but he has to make do with what there is. This is a sensible, tactical reaction to a totally unexpected situation. No panic. He spent a while picking out not just a spanner but probably the biggest spanner, the most formidable spanner. His mind is functioning well. No collapse. Now, he's doing a systematic search, room by room. Again, no panic. There's a big chance he'll be able to convince himself that the filthy slur in "Panicking Ralph" or "Panicking Ralphy" is all wrong. He's always believed that. This proves it. Others must agree now. He's showing bravery, coolness, method. He's Ralph W. Ember. No corruption of that name is allowed, no demeaning additions.'

'Well, perhaps you're right,' Harpur said. He wasn't sure Ralph would accept this analysis, but it did make sense. Ralph hated to be thought a poltroon. His spanner declared he wasn't. Grand, Ralph!

She took off the bowler hat and placed the pistol on top of her head, carefully, emphatically. Then she put the hat back on over it and pulled the bowler down hard so, as before, it rested on her ears. The gun caused bumps in the outline of the bowler, but Harpur felt this didn't matter because few people would expect an automatic pistol to be under a bowler hat on a woman's head in the small hours and were unlikely to notice. And, in any case, there were no people other than Harpur to see the bowler. 'I need my hands free for the climb,' she said.

'Climb?'

'The ladder.'

'Absolutely no need for you to go up the ladder.' Harpur spoke urgently.

'No need, no, but I want to see what you were doing up there.'

'I've told you. The boards. Nails.'

'You've told me shit,' she replied. She took hold of the handrails and began to ascend. She went slowly. Harpur could tell that the rungs hurt her bare feet. But she kept going. The bowler stayed in place. Although there was a breeze that ruffled the nightdress, she remained more or less decent. Harpur put a foot on the ladder's lowest rung to steady it and looked anywhere but at her. Pyjamas would have been more convenient for Margaret's kind of present behaviour. However, Harpur did realize that she could not have foreseen the sudden need for arse modesty on a ladder by night. It was luck that the gun fitted OK for size under the bowler. Manufacturers of the pistol could not possibly have envisaged this kind of requirement.

Lights upstairs in the house began to come on, the sequence moving fairly fast towards the east wing. Outside, Margaret had reached the first floor and didn't need to grip the ladder once she had finished going up. She was ferreting about up there. Harpur allowed himself a glance at her now. She took off the bowler with her left hand and very gingerly with the right retrieved the gun. She put the bowler back on and then pointed the gun towards a full moon and fired two shots into the air. 'Yippee!' she blurted, chortling at maximum power.

She put her face close to the boards up there and shouted: 'Hear that, Ralph? This way, darling. It's OK, we're here. Welcome home. Not ill met by moonlight but brilliantly.'

A pause. Inside, Ralph must have been moving towards the masonry gap. Then his voice came loud enough through the planks for Harpur to hear. 'Why?' Ralph said.

'Why what?' Margaret said.

'Why are you there?'

'So courageous, Ralph,' she replied. 'So devoted to our cause.'

'Who?'

'You,' Margaret said.

'No, I mean who is with you? I think I heard you say "we".'

'Harpur.'

'Harpur?'

'The Super Dick.'

'Why?'

'He was up the ladder.'

'What ladder?' Ralph said.

'The ladder for the extension work. I'm on it now. These things come in handy if one wants to get to the roof.'

'Well, yes clearly. But why was Harpur up the ladder?'

'Who fucking knows?' she said.

'Have you asked him?'

'He says routine,' she replied.

'How can it be routine?' Ralph said.

'Exactly,' she said. 'I put that to him.'

'Basic, Ralph,' Harpur said.

'Did Iles force you to get up the ladder, Harpur,' Ralph replied.

'I've already asked him if it's to do with Iles,' Margaret said.

'It's the kind of thing Iles would love,' Ralph said.

'Which kind?' Margaret said.

'Ladders and so on,' Ralph said.

'I don't know of any previous incident involving Mr Iles and ladders,' Harpur said. 'We have to be very accurate if we're speculating about personal qualities.'

'I mean ladders in a general sense,' Ralph said.

'General how?' Harpur said.

'That kind of thing – ladders now, but also other types of things,' Ralph replied.

'Which other types?' Margaret said.

'Unusual things,' Ralph said.

'Ladders aren't unusual on a building site,' Harpur said.

'But in a certain context,' Ralph said.

'Which?' Harpur replied.

'This one,' Ralph said.

'Hello!' Margaret said. 'Guess who's leaving the house? It's Venetia. I've got a great view of things from up here. You must have woken her, Ralph. Were you looking for me in the kids' bedrooms?'

Harpur, below, had also seen someone, lit up by the porch light, emerge from the front door of Low Pastures and begin walking towards him and the ladder and the shouting and gun noise. With that help from Margaret, he could make out it was one of Ember's daughters. She seemed to have on training shoes and a football club tunic, red and black stripes, reaching her ankles. Light through the uncurtained downstairs windows helped make things clearer now.

'It's OK, darling,' Margaret told her. 'Mr Harpur had to do some checks. Routine.'

'Mr Harpur?' Venetia replied.

'He's police,' Margaret said.

'What checks?'

'Up here and below,' Margaret said.

'But what?' Venetia said.

'Yes,' Margaret said.

'Just routine,' Harpur said. Margaret took the bowler off and replaced the gun securely on her head, then put the hat back on, freeing her hands. She began to come down the ladder.

Harpur heard a car travelling fast and approaching the house. Its headlights were on main beam as it accelerated up the drive, the sound of tyres on gravel at first, then smoother, on tarmac. The Volvo pulled up behind Ralph's Mercedes near the porch. The driver's door of the Volvo was pushed violently open. Tracy rolled out and in one quick movement folded down into a sniper's crouch pointing a Glock semi-automatic at Margaret on the ladder. 'Armed police!' Tracy howled. 'Armed police. Don't move. Drop any weapon.'

'I can't yet,' Margaret said.

'Can't what?' Ralph said through the boarding.

Roy Verity-Wright also left the Volvo. He had no gun but stood alongside their car. 'We heard shots,' he said. 'Two.'

'The gun's under her bowler,' Harpur told Tracy. 'Because of the ladder.'

'How do you mean, Mr Harpur?' Roy said.

'In which respect?' Harpur replied.

'"Because of the ladder",' Roy said.

'She needed something to grip,' Harpur said.

'Women do,' Margaret said.

Tracy straightened and lowered the Glock. 'Did Mr Iles arrange all this, sir?' she said.

'That question keeps coming up,' Harpur said.

'I don't understand what's happening,' Verity-Wright said.

'Really?' Margaret replied.

She had reached the ground. Tracy raised the Glock and

pointed it at Margaret again. 'Stay where you are,' Tracy said. 'Put your gun on the floor and step back one pace from it. Roy will approach and recover your gun.'

Margaret bent to put the gun on the floor. She moved backwards away from it.

'OK Roy,' Tracy said.

He did as Tracy had ordered. He picked up Margaret's gun and went to stand by Tracy with it. Tracy lowered her Glock and took the pistol from Roy. She put it in a pocket. Harpur retracted the ladder's extra length and then brought it down and replaced it with the others.

Ralph came out from the main entrance to the house. He'd obviously realized that the search inside was pointless. He walked quickly to Margaret and kissed her on the cheek. She handed him his bowler. But he laughed and put it back on her head and down to her ears. 'Fashion,' he said. She didn't remove it this time. 'Your poor dear bare feet,' he said.

Another car, an Audi, entered the drive at a gentle speed and stopped near the Volvo. Iles got out. He was in plain clothes – one of his suave suits, a red cravat on an open-necked blue shirt, grey woollen slacks and desert boots. 'The folk at Apsley Farm called to report a lot of late-night activity at Low Pastures,' he said. 'Knowing my abiding interest in and affection for Low Pastures and its family, the Control Room rang me, despite the hour. And then en route did I hear gunshots? I stopped for a while and looked about. Nothing, though.'

'Just to let Ralph know where I was,' Margaret said.

'That would be vital,' Iles said.

'We've done a good examination of the planks up and down,' Margaret said. 'They're fine. Couldn't be stauncher.'

'You're lucky,' Iles replied. 'It's improbable that you'll ever find anyone more accomplished at examining planks up or down than Col. Show him a plank and he'll purr like a she-cat. There's a note about it on his CV. In the space for Special Interests, it says "Planks".'

'Everything here is normal, sir,' Harpur said.

'Normal?' Roy Verity-Wright said.

SIX

R alph concentrated on watching himself approach the house carrying that good-sized spanner. If spanners could be iconic, this one was what the present spanner was. There was a deep, almost mystical rightness about this combination, the spanner and him. As spanners went, it might seem quite ordinary, but Ralph couldn't think of it as like that. By taking the spanner with him in this specific way – flourished near an open door of a terrific house – he was turning it into a special kind of spanner, chosen very selectively from a car boot.

It would have been the same no matter who was carrying it to the house, as long as the intended purpose was the same, though Ralph did feel that because it was he, Ralph W. Ember, bearing the spanner, sometimes with two hands, sometimes the right only, this gave it not merely a special status but something extra special within that special status, like special status squared.

CCTV covered the porch area of Low Pastures, and in the Entertainment Suite at Low Pastures he privately ran that sequence of the film a few times. It showed him arriving in the Mercedes, then opening the driver's door as if about to get out immediately, but pausing with his body slewed to leave the car seat and his feet on the ground, while he stared towards the open front door of the house. At that hour, as Ralph or anyone else would have expected, it was a startled stare, though. He remembered exclaiming, 'Where the fuck are they?' Ralph lip-read that now on the film.

He gladly noted that the resemblance to Charlton Heston remained intact, and if anything was an improvement – strong but less craggy, gentler. Maybe gentleness wasn't the kind of looks you needed if you were going to win a chariot race, which was what Chuck did, of course, in his film, *Ben Hur*, standing right up close to horses' rears. But Ralph had different needs. Anyway, it was probably his stand-in who did the race.

This pause by him, part out of the Mercedes, part in, was brief. He considered it definitely had not indicated paralysis through fear. No! Ralph considered it a pause of someone wisely taking several moments while he adjusted to a quite unexpected situation: the front door open and unattended at around 4 a.m. Second thoughts.

Perhaps aided by memory, Ralph could read in his face on the screen a calm resolve to deal with this problem head-on. The word 'undaunted' buzzed in his brain but he tried to dismiss it as overblown and vain. 'Staunch': that was how he'd describe himself as he left the driving seat and walked quickly to the rear of the car and opened the boot: important for the walk to be quick and decisive, this was commitment. Naturally, he'd known that the camera would be on him. He absolutely had to go through with his plan to find a weapon and get armed, otherwise he would be a nothing, a showboat. It didn't matter that he might be the only one who saw the film. The shame would still savage him. There were times when Ralph had the idea he might actually *be* a bit of a showboat, and he didn't want that idea in any way, or to any amount, increased. It was bound to be a hazard when someone had achieved so much and meant to go on achieving. Part of the justified reward for success was recognition of that success by others.

There might be indentations in the metal at the handle end of the spanner to help someone's grip – Ralph's, on that occasion. This had heartened him as he drew it from the boot and he could see that satisfaction in Ralph's features on the film. 'Come to me', they seemed to say, so warmly to the potential, resting bludgeon. The satisfaction was limited, of course. After all, the spanner was only a spanner, even a Mercedes spanner. It could be used as a weapon but was not actually a weapon. That is, it was not a gun. Its function was with bolts. Some would describe it as hopelessly not a gun. They'd regard this situation as the sort Chuck Heston had envisaged when he said that citizens should have the total right to defend themselves with a firearm.

Ralph did own guns, but only very rarely carried one. An evening and night catering for Intelligent Percy's triumphant do at the club hadn't seemed that kind of occasion. One thing Intelligent was intelligent about was not getting drawn into gunfire turf battles. It would have been different if he'd been called 'Clever Percy' or 'Smart Percy'. These words did contain praise but they also suggested a sort of short-term craftiness. *Intelligent* Percy always went for a wide, thorough view of things and behaved with restraint, at least until violence became in his personal estimate inevitable.

And so Ralph had realized that he might have to take on people with guns though he had only a spanner, probably with an indented shaft. What did 'take on' mean here? It had meant get close enough to any intruders to do effective damage with a swinging spanner. And, next, what did 'effective' mean? It meant landing at least one full power blow before shots could be fired. No guarantee. Bullets might stop him and the spanner while they were still nearing at a harmless distance, the way big-game hunters might stop a charging lion. Ralph didn't like this comparison in all its aspects, of course, but he did favour the nature and guts of the lion, even though the animal was doomed.

He felt the spanner deserved better than this. It wasn't any old spanner, or even any old big spanner. Tools were kept in a multi-pocket rack most likely, and it had taken him a full minute to select the most suitable one for a set-to. Although he had walked so swiftly to the boot, speed in actually picking this brilliantly specific spanner would have been an error. The boot had bright internal lighting and this, plus the porch bulb, helped make his choice the right one. He closed the boot and the driver's door very quietly, though he'd realized at the time that these precautions might be pointless because any enemies in the house would certainly have heard the Mercedes arrive. His behaviour had been more or less automatic.

The shock of the open door must have crushed his thinking powers. But, looking back now from where he sat in the Entertainment Suite, he felt that – although his actions then were not completely sensible – he'd known he must try to control the situation somehow, and do what was possible. The thought that people in the house might have heard him draw up had troubled Ralph badly at the time. It meant, didn't it, that they could be ready for him, might be waiting for him? He'd appear spotlighted and framed in the door space when he entered Low Pastures. Somehow – and he didn't altogether understand that somehow – somehow, he'd forced himself to keep going, and he'd walked doggedly into the dark house. He'd feared Margaret and the children might be in danger and he had an undodgeable duty to protect them. Bravery would occasionally take over Ralph, despite himself, especially when it was a matter of family, Low Pastures or the club. 'Courage', wasn't it, that Churchill said was the most desirable quality in a man or woman – because it made the others possible.

Ralph had also realized at the time that if nobody came out of the house to discover who had just turned up, despite these engine and tyre sounds, it could prove there was nobody in the house who shouldn't be. Hell, he'd hated this interpretation of things. Didn't it negate his valour? He didn't go in for valour very much, and when he did he wanted it nicely treated. Of course, there had been another possible reason for nobody appearing from the house. Ralph hadn't liked to dwell on it. He hadn't definitely known there was anyone alive in the property.

Overall, Ralph knew what irritated him most about the incident at Low Pastures. It was that he never seemed to start anything, initiate something. Wasn't he always following up what had been said or done by someone else? He *re*acted because someone had acted, had prompted him so forcibly. He didn't know what the opposite of proactive was, but he often felt like he might be it. This seemed to Ralph a poor sort of role for someone of his unquenchable creative flair – a flair that pointed him towards The Monty's splendid potential and glistening promise.

Looking at himself now on this film, Ralph could see no evidence of flair. He had been pushed – compelled, dragooned – into stalking supposed enemies with a spanner. The initiative was totally theirs, if they existed. He had to respond, and not elegantly. They set up the situation and he had to deal with it, try to deal with it.

The CCTV film couldn't follow him into the house. Memory had to do. He'd switched lights on and eye-searched first what Margaret and he called the Round Room, because of its two curved walls. They generally ate here. It had a four-leaf mahogany table, a mahogany chiffonier, six straight-backed dining chairs, a chesterfield in dark red moquette. Ralph was very fond of chesterfields. Their fat arms seemed to promise a welcome, and a specific kind of sit-down. The room had, too, four big Edwardian or Victorian armchairs, also in dark red moquette. It had naturally been one of the ground-floor rooms he'd searched first when he thought Margaret and the children missing. He'd been scared but enraged as well: it seemed so disgraceful that someone, or more than one, should get into Ralph's personal, elite home, and contemptuously menace his family – contemptuously and contemptibly.

Upstairs, when he'd looked in at their bedroom and switched on the lights there, he saw that Margaret was absent, though her side of the bed had obviously been occupied at some time tonight. Next he'd checked the children's rooms. Both were sleeping. The difference had confused him, increased his anxieties: only his wife targeted, why?

But 'targeted'? Margaret had a mind and a will, didn't she? Had she decided for herself to go? Had she planned something like this, carried out something like this? These thoughts and others similar had begun to pile up in Ralph's brain. He'd desperately asked himself where was she and why and how was she where she was? And was she alone? If not, who was with her?

And after another moment or two, he'd had an answer to these queries. She was outside at the east end of the property, apparently up a ladder. There was what sounded to him like gunfire – two shots – and then Margaret yelled, 'Yippee!'

It wasn't a word he'd ever heard from Margaret before, bu he recognized her voice at once. Soon after, she called hi name. It sounded as though she had put her mouth close t the boards the builders used to seal off temporarily any ga caused by their day's work. 'Hear that, Ralph, dear?' she said. She'd meant the gunshots. She'd sounded proud them, as though they indicated splendid high spirits. This h

infuriated Ralph and still did. She had been trying to make a foolish joke of this situation whereas he had been deeply, oh, very deeply, suffering, half crushed by Fate and intolerable mystery. It was heartless of her – flippant, mocking.

Ralph found that reminiscing about this episode brought too much pain. He left his den in the Entertainment Suite and went out into the grounds of Low Pastures. He needed to see the solidity, the quiet sureness and strength of the building as a correction of all those intolerable memories. Instead of Margaret up one of the ladders and behaving outrageously last night, that damn nightdress fluttering so trivializingly in the wind, there was now a workman climbing expertly from the ladder on to the roof to do some re-slating needed for the new join between two parts of the house. The boards were no longer in use but stacked tidily near the foot of the ladder. To Ralph this was a scene of serious progress, not a site for random gunfire and daft shouting. Had she been drinking?

The man up the ladder called out: 'All coming along very nicely, Ralph. You'll have a grand extension of floor space, to be filled with objects of real beauty. Many congrats, I'm sure. No wonder Low Pastures is spoken of so admiringly, and that will certainly continue when these improvements are complete.' Ralph didn't mind them using his first name, or talking as though they were partners not hired labour. They were doing the job and adding to the prestige of Low Pastures. That's what counted. This was a property that spoke of present success and of a magnificent history. He was the custodian of both, and a guarantee for the future. This was not, repeat not, the kind of achievement that could be summed up in a screeched, 'Yippee!'

SEVEN

A stranger, or strangers, would occasionally turn up at Harpur's house in Arthur Street wanting to discuss something urgent – in their eyes urgent, at least. Harpur didn't always agree, but he would generally try to give a sympathetic listening. After all, he more or less invited these visits. He'd never gone in for anonymity, though most detectives did. His name and address were in all the directories. It was a bit of a pious fetish with him: he believed that if someone had bad trouble and needed help, Harpur should be available, supposing help was possible. Iles regarded it as lunacy, a kind of self-punishment, but Harpur was totally stuck with this awkward, compulsive sense of duty. Iles referred to it as 'Old Ma Harpur's Comfort Corner'. Generally speaking, Harpur could put up with – ignore – this kind of mockery from Iles or anyone else. Now and then, though, it irritated him, might make him wonder if he still had the right temperament for modern policing. It could even make him think occasionally about early retirement. Very briefly he had discussed that prospect with his daughters. He'd floated the idea with them of quitting the Force and launching himself as a private investigator. Hazel had been very hostile – said he wasn't the right sort for that kind of career. She insisted that he needed a structure for him to operate inside of, and only a police force provided that. Harpur half agreed with her and the plans had been dropped – didn't really get as far as plans: half-baked urges.

'Well, hello, my dear. You must be one of his, your name being . . .?'

'Jill,' Jill said. As often happened she had responded faster than Harpur to the doorbell. He stood behind her now in the hallway, not part of the conversation, or not part yet. He didn't recognize the woman outside, and it was obvious Jill didn't know her, either. She would be late twenties, very cared-for teeth and complexion, grey-blue eyes, white, about five foot ten or eleven, and the proper weight for that. She had on what Harpur thought to be a brilliantly expensive, pinstripe, London navy suit, as fine a piece of work as the dead man's. Jill had taken a stance that barred the woman's way into the house, but Jill's voice sounded welcoming.

As happened now and then with Harpur, his mind would lock on to something or some things that appeared fairly trivial and make it or them grounds for what might turn out to be important positive guesswork. The similar tailoring did that today, plus the woman's London accent. He thought this caller was in some way linked to the man he'd found dead at the wharf. It hadn't taken long to identify the corpse and Harpur had put Chief Inspector Garland to investigate the crime. The dead man was Lawrence Ilk Masel from Enfield, a London district. The Metropolitan Police had no knowledge of him, other than the death.

'It's my dad you want, I expect,' Jill said at the front porch. 'We get quite a few people looking for him, don't we, Dad?' Graciously, she turned her head a little to draw Harpur into the meeting, as long as he could keep up.

'Some people do, yes,' Harpur said.

'It's usually about his job,' Jill said. 'Police so far.'

'Yes, his job,' the woman said.

'There are many sides to his job,' Jill said. 'All sorts.'

'Yes, I expect so. But it's just one of them that interests me,' the woman said.

'It's true about most of the people who call,' Jill said. 'They have a simple topic that is troubling them.' Hazel joined them in the porch.

'I'd have guessed as much,' the woman said.

'Some of it is confidential.'

'Yes,' the woman said.

'He won't be able to talk to you about that,' Jill replied. 'I think you should understand this so as not to be disappointed. He'll do whatever he can but there are boundaries imposed by the situation. He'll say the inquiries are "ongoing". This is one of those police words – "ongoing". If an inquiry is ongoing, it means that nobody who is not a cop will be allowed a true sniff of it. In fact the inquiries might not be ongoing at all, but they can't admit that because it would make them look lazy and stupid.

'Or then there's "at this juncture". He or one of his team will say, "We cannot disclose further information at this juncture." Of course, that makes it sound like although they can't reveal anything at this juncture, meaning now, there'll be other junctures in the future and the information will be available at this later juncture, so all that's required is patience and the ability to spot the kind of juncture that will be helpful. There are plenty of junctures floating about. Some people believe what they're told about junctures, some don't.'

'Right,' the woman said.

'I'm sure you knew that was his job.'

'Yes.'

'Or you wouldn't be here,' Jill said.

'It's definitely the police side of things I wanted to discuss,' the woman said.

'He doesn't do Traffic or lost dogs or anything like that. Those are other departments. Dad hardly ever wears a uniform. He's a detective, detective chief superintendent, and he spends his time finding out things that were hidden. Investigations, they're called. Most of the time he tries not to seem like police. This is why he doesn't wear a uniform. He can merge with the population. He digs.'

'That's what I want,' the woman said.

'Sometimes we can help Dad – that is, help Dad help the person he is doing his best to help, because sometimes his best is not the kind of best needed, isn't good enough. No, I've got that wrong. It's because he is coming from another era. Things are different. It's sad, really. I believe it depresses him, makes him think he should try a different kind of life. New for him.'

'I'm sure he appreciates your efforts,' the woman said.

'The female angle,' Jill replied. 'We can give him some of that. His girlfriend called Denise has plenty of it, but she's not always here, owing to being a student with a lot of friends. Maybe we'd be able to help him help you, for instance. There used to be our mother also to show the female angle. But she's not here now, either.'

'I heard about that,' the woman said.

'Murdered.[3] It had something to do with an investigation.'

'Yes.'

'And also youth,' Jill replied.

'Youth?'

'Although Dad's not old – you're not old are you, Dad?' She turned her face towards him again. 'He's not young, either. Pension in sight. So, we can let him know any youth stuff. Guidance. That's me and my sister, Hazel. I mentioned an era just now.'

'I'm not youth,' the woman said.

'No, but you are young, youngish,' Jill said.

'So far,' the woman replied.

'When we're talking like this, I'm sorry to call you just "you". I don't know your name. "You" sounds so cold,' Jill said.

'Rebecca.'

'It's a Bible name, isn't it?' Hazel said.

'What?'

'Rebecca in the Old Testament. Dad knows the Bible. His parents made him go to Sunday school, although he didn't want to,' Hazel said.

'Rebecca was the wife of Isaac, mother of Jacob,' Harpur said.

'There,' Jill said.

'We generally spell it with two cc's in the middle, the Bible with a k,' Harpur said. He decided it was time to stop Jill, and now Hazel as well, trundling on in that style of hers.

'I have a feeling you're here about a man found dead at the sand and gravel wharf in the docks, Lawrence Ilk Masel,' he said. He eased Jill aside so he could speak more directly to the visitor.

'Yes,' she said. 'Clever of you.'

'There are times when Dad can be clever,' Jill said. 'This murder has been in the papers and on telly.' She grasped Harpur's arm. 'But, dad, aren't we terribly rude to be keeping

<hr>

[3] See *Roses, Roses.*

Rebecca out in the porch like she was some nuisance sales person?'

'*Very* rude,' Harpur said.

'You knew the dead man, did you, Rebecca?' Hazel said.

'We were close.'

This kind of front-door vetting was a procedure the girls had used before. If one of them answered the doorbell before him they'd do a sort of scrutiny routine on the stranger, trying to work out whether it was the kind of caller who could be useful to their father, or only a possible gabby nuisance. There were enough of those available. Not everyone who came made it into the house. But Jill stood aside now, tugging Harpur with her, and the woman stepped past them. Harpur pointed through the open door of the house towards the sitting room, inviting Rebecca in. But she said: 'I have this fierce need. I'd like to go now, immediately, to see where it happened to him. I'm sorry if I sound demanding and impatient. But perhaps you'll understand.'

'Of course we do,' Jill said. 'Yes, yes. Dad will drive us, won't you, Dad?'

'It all looks so cosy in the sitting room, but I'm not here for cosiness.'

Hazel suddenly went out to the middle of the little lawn in front of the house. She arranged herself into what Harpur thought must be a ballet stance on her toes, arms above her head and stretched upwards. They did some ballet exercises at school. She performed a slow spin, a big, exuberant smile on her face. It was as if she had an enthusiastic audience, not just Rebecca, Harpur and Jill. Harpur felt deeply surprised. Hazel was not normally an exhibitionist. There were times, in fact, when she looked formidably stern, especially stern for a child.

'I depict contentment,' Hazel said. 'That room you glimpsed, Rebecca, is what people are looking for. It brings satisfaction, happiness, restfulness.'

'Which people?' Jill said.

'People looking for somewhere comfortable, tranquil.'

'Like me?' Rebecca said.

'I'm sorry to say so, but yes,' Hazel said. 'It tells them they are on the right track. This room is part of that peace and quiet pleasure, and is part of why Rebecca is here. Nothing against you for that, Rebecca, absolutely nothing at all. Only sensible. But it will give you a taste for it, won't it?'

Jill said: 'And her . . . well, ex-boyfriend was the same.'

'Right then, I think we ought to go and see the site,' Harpur said. 'That's probably why Rebecca has come from London. Well, she has said as much.' One of his daughters had invited Rebecca – or more or less invited her – into the house; the other had laid on a stage show for her. Harpur thought them wonderful assets.

'I want to see personally how matters are going – the investigation,' Rebecca said. 'I fear things might be developing as they have in other big cities. The drugs trade has taken over. These are new conditions, not happy ones. Was my dead friend trapped in them? It's a very scary notion.'

Harpur drove the four of them to the docks. Another dredger was moored at the same sand and gravel wharf as when he'd found the body. A ten-foot-high pyramid of sand stood near the ship, ready for distribution by truck to building works somewhere, maybe at Ralph's. It was the kind of commerce Harpur understood and sympathized with.

While they watched from the car, three teenage boys began to play around the sand heap, flinging handfuls at one another. One of them did an imitation stagger of how someone might collapse if just about to die from a shooting. He fell face down into the sand. The others giggled and hooted. In its addled way, the childish moment of corny theatricals comforted Harpur. For cities much accustomed to murders, there would not be any point in mocking someone's death performance: mickey-taking of it would be no more than farce. Gross, doomed farce. Perhaps Rebecca was used to that kind of cruel gig. Rebecca got out of the car and approached them, but said nothing. Soon, Hazel came and stood alongside her. She took a light grip on Rebecca's shoulder. Neither spoke. The boy in the sand twitched a bit like death throes, setting off little grubby rivulets near his knees and his jaw.

Harpur drove them back with Rebecca alongside him in the

passenger seat. He thought she had become sort of sheepish. 'But look, I'm not sure I should be saying this – not sure at all.' She made her voice big and plonkish. 'Is there free speech here?'

'It sounds to me like it could be helpful, whatever it is,' Jill said. 'Doesn't it seem to you, Dad, that Rebecca might have something quite helpful to tell us.'

'Certainly,' Harpur said.

'Kindly of you to say so,' Rebecca said. 'But I wondered if you knew it already.'

'Know it already?' Hazel said.

'Which?' Jill said.

'Which bits of it do you think Dad knows already?'

'He is from a sort who know a lot without showing,' Jill said. 'That's how police are, blank as blank, but they'll bring an item out suddenly, give you a shock, put you off balance. They have to deal with real hard people who won't talk. So police must find a way to shake them. Which bits of it are you thinking of when you say he knows it already?'

'Everything,' Rebecca replied.

'He'll listen for a while to you or Haze or me and won't interrupt in case buried here or there is a little fragment that is not new, not mentioned before. Crafty. Careful. No waste,' Jill said. 'Or it will be something we don't see the true importance of.'

'Sitting on stuff,' Rebecca said.

'Are you sitting on stuff, Dad?' Jill said. 'We know that sometimes you do, because you want to get one up on Des Iles. It's like a game, such as chess.'

'Not that kind of stuff,' Rebecca said.

'Which kind?' Hazel said.

'I have a notion that someone might be watching me,' Rebecca said, 'at the place where I've got bed and breakfast. And perhaps your dad knows of this.'

Jill said: 'Did you have that already, Dad – someone keeping an eye on Rebecca?'

'We didn't know about Rebecca until she called here today,' Harpur said.

'There's not much to know,' Rebecca said. 'Lawrence and

I didn't live together. Nothing like that. I'd seen him only a few times. It's so bleak and awful. There was no reason for the police to contact me, London police or the local police here. He interested me, though. I wanted to find out why he finished up at the docks wharf. I recognized his name from the news reports and the town's name, of course. Then, chatting to some people I met on the train and in the bed-and-breakfast, I heard of a Mr Harpur, top detective, and where he lived. I picked up hints that it might be Mr Harpur who found the body in that grim place. And so I arrive on your doorstep. I wondered – wonder – whether this city was going the same way as other big cities in Britain and slipping towards anarchy because of the drugs trade. I ask again, how did Lawrence get caught up in something like that?'

'That's enough of this kind of conversation,' Harpur said.

'Which kind?' Jill said.

'Going nowhere,' Harpur said.

'So, why?'

'Why what?' Harpur said.

Hazel said: 'Why is it going nowhere? Why so daft and stupid – the chat about Rebecca's names and so on. It all sounded very silly.' Occasionally Hazel and Jill would form an aggressive alliance. It wasn't only Jill who could get tough.

'I have to feel my way,' Rebecca said.

Jill said: 'We'd help you, wouldn't we, Dad, but not with something that makes no sense.'

'Well, try,' Harpur said.

'Was it you who found the body, Dad?' Hazel said.

'It's the kind of thing Dad wouldn't tell us, Rebecca, but never mind, we still would like to assist. And I think this could be handy, couldn't it, Dad?' Jill said.

'Handy?' Harpur replied.

'You know what I mean,' Jill said.

And, yes, he did have an idea of what she meant.

'On a plate,' Jill said. 'Kind of an exercise in the new career.'

Rebecca said: 'On a plate?'

'Jill gets quite a few notions,' Harpur said.

'This is not some new notion,' Jill said.

'Oh?' Harpur said.

'We sort of discussed it,' Jill said.

'Sort of? Which sort of?' Harpur said.

'When you said you were thinking of retirement,' Jill replied.

'Just a dream,' Harpur said, 'a bit of escapism.'

'That's not how it sounded,' Jill said.

'No? It should have,' Harpur said. 'Quite a few people my age and rank are considering it.'

'And didn't you say you might turn yourself into a private investigator? But Hazel thinks you wouldn't be much good at it because you will have forgotten all the basic skills, being shut up in your office most of the time,' Jill said.

'Hazel can be rather difficult and snotty,' Harpur replied. 'She'd like to be kind but now and then gets tough.'

'Well, here's your chance to show you can still do it,' Jill said.

'Still do what?' Harpur asked.

'Simple but necessary things for an investigation – such as tailing. There's this man hanging about Rebecca's temporary place. Could you get behind him and find out who he is and what he's doing? Important. This is connected to the murder, isn't it? It would have to be secret. Could you do it, Dad?' Jill said.

To Harpur's mind there were unquestionably some skills of his trade that he no longer performed perfectly, including undetected tracking of a target suspect. Jill and Hazel were right, it was not a knack that someone of his present rank needed to use much now, and the ability had dwindled.

'Can you be sure Rebecca's all right?' Jill said. 'Is she safe? Are things in this city turning very dark because of the drugs industry? That's what some kids in school say – like London or Manchester.'

No, true enough. Harpur certainly could not be sure Rebecca was safe. Perhaps Jill's classroom pals might have things right and the city was sliding towards a terrible similarity to other major places where districts might be ruled by villainy. Rebecca worried about Lawrence's possible connection with drugs firms, and now Harpur had to worry about Rebecca's possible involvement, too.

'We're aware of that danger from outside,' Harpur said.

'"Aware of", but what does that mean, Dad – aware of but not trying to stop it,' Jill said.

'Or doing nothing much,' Hazel added. 'Tolerating. It's Iles's soft option, isn't it?'

'I wouldn't say that,' Harpur told them.

'No, I repeat, we know you wouldn't say it, but that's how it is, tactically unspoken and accepted,' Hazel said.

'Dad will fight it, won't you Dad?' Jill said.

'We'll see,' Hazel replied. 'There's this phrase around a lot lately – "proactive". It's what you're not, isn't it?'

'I'm trying to find the truth and how Lawrence became a part of the darkness,' Rebecca said.

Harpur wondered whether Rebecca realized she was perhaps becoming part of the darkness herself? It took only one step. Had she already taken it?

EIGHT

And so, Harpur tried some undercover tracking. For this there were two motives. In some ways these were extremely different, in some others, though, very similar. They were both about how to cater for a disturbingly unclear future. One of these unclear futures was Harpur's. Would he retire, would he try to establish himself as a private investigator when his official time was over? A month or two ago, that would have been a preposterous suggestion. Not now.

There was also a much wider, unclear future – this city's moral health, endangered moral health. He wanted to see whether he had the kind of smartness necessary for a private detective. He wanted also to uncover and deal with the threats to the wholesomeness and safety of this police patch and the area in general. He realized this must come across as a rather worthy, self-righteous notion, but he would need that kind of motivation.

Harpur reckoned the start of this operation had got off well. Rebecca had given him her bed-and-breakfast address and a good description of the unknown figure she thought was watching the property and her. He was about thirty, slight, mid-height, white, fair haired, usually wearing a black leather jacket and navy cord trousers, carrying a holdall today.

The bed-and-breakfast was part of an ordinary Victorian or Edwardian large house. There was quite a lot of activity in the street, people setting off to work and on other journeys, but Harpur thought he identified correctly the one who interested Rebecca and therefore him. That was comparatively simple. What was not so simple was Harpur's objective. What did he expect to find if he was led somewhere by this character? He remembered from distant training in surveillance, as it was called then, any project of this kind must have one definite and obvious aim. He couldn't see one here.

Of course, Harpur had realized when starting this operation

unaided, that on a properly managed and resourced official police tailing job, there would have been six or more plain-clothes officers involved, with changes every half-hour or so to make sure the target didn't notice a constant figure in his/her steady slipstream. The figure was variable, but his/her role was not. He/she was known as 'eyeball' and must not lose sight of the target. After a due stint another of the team would replace her/him – a very orderly procedure.

But Harpur's now was no carefully managed police tailing job. Nothing like. He had to work very much on his own. He'd come to feel he must deal with it solo, regardless of whether he might retire. The mission couldn't be divided into slices, one officer taking a portion, then handing over to the next until all the pieces were completed. Perhaps there would be no nicely rounded-off conclusion for Harpur. There was no 'next' to hand over to, or rather, he was next, just as he'd been before.

But he'd decided he couldn't let his daughters down, especially Hazel. He had to repair – in person, absolutely in person – their sad, complete collapse of confidence in him. That meant he must handle this situation unsupported. At times, Harpur suspected his daughters were protecting him, guarding him, not the reverse – he protecting and guarding them. They seemed to regard him as a liability. This he could not live with and needed to correct. Personally. They had one parent only. This brought special respon-sibilities. He knew his daughters would have regarded it as farcical if he'd let them see how seriously he took fatherhood, so he'd hide it. He concentrated on reviving ancient, neglected aptitudes. As far as was feasible, he'd take over the leadership of this project. And he had to make it feasible, make whatever changes were required.

He'd heard that Ralph Ember spent quite a lot of his energy fighting off slurs. Weirdly, Harpur felt a kind of major bond with this prime crook, though Ember's problems dated quite a way back, and Harpur's were emphatically now, and in the family home, and/or six yards behind a fast-moving, leather-jacketed, still almost youthful stranger who apparently had such an obvious interest in where Rebecca lodged. Harpur had decided he must have a go at it. Six yards had been the distance recommended in those training sessions – not too close, and therefore easy to spot, and not too far off, and therefore easy to lose.

Hazel saw things very shrewdly: it was a long time since Harpur had needed to follow someone and stay unseen. He had to revive this complex skill and other complex skills, if he could. Harpur thought both his daughters approved of what he was doing – going it alone. Denise agreed. There had been discussions.

'I think it will all come back to you once you begin,' Denise had said. 'Like with a foreign language unused for a while, but now called upon. I believe in you. The girls believe in you.'

'It's not exactly like reviving a foreign language, though, is it? If you get this wrong you might get shot, Dad,' Jill had said. 'Just the same, you think he should do it, Haze, do you?'

'It's a balance – is the danger worth the risk because of what Dad might learn,' Hazel said. 'I'm not as much against as I was.'

'If you feel it's going haywire, Dad, drop it, pull out – at once, pull out. The risk is too much for what Dad might get. Might. Very much and only, might,' Jill said.

Harpur knew he had to be very careful. He mustn't let the tailing job become an obsession. That kind of mega-attention could take over the face and possibly physique of an officer doing a clandestine tail. This proved there was acute focus on the operation and in some ways was a big plus; but also it might function so effectively that it became noticeable, a kind of deadpan but the wrong kind. It displayed an unduly intent interest in the target just ahead. There was a good chance it would tell the quarry he or she had a tail. An undercover officer's unwavering commitment to the shadowing task could betray this special purpose, not just in the blank face, but also in the unrelaxed, dogged, crouched body. Harpur had to avoid getting a tailing operation brilliantly under way, but to such a degree that it drew hostile notice. He had to avoid, also, instinctively falling into flagrant step with the target. This might suggest a kind of robot intimacy and would invite unwanted attention.

Shops. Oh God, shops. They were among shops now. Big shops, especially, brought hellish snags. There had been a lot about these in those early training sessions and Harpur now could see why. He half-remembered surveillance exercises when the officer playing the target would suddenly disappear into one of a shop's wide doorways and merge unfindably with the crowd of customers. Harpur hated supermarkets, then, and found he still did today when the tailing seemed stuck.

And there were added new drawbacks. Glassware as part of a shopfront's decoration seemed more common these days and could produce, all at once, unexpected mirror images, perhaps of the trailer's head and face. It would be unintended, an accident, but it could happen, and happen repeatedly. The target was certain to become aware of it, so Harpur knew he had to be ever ready to get an arm up to act as mask.

Harpur, still achieving no real progress so far today, saw another reason, maybe more powerful and definitely a bit pathetic, for getting his arm up fast and into a blocking out position: yes, didn't some of these reflections today make him look old; not just old but resignedly, almost cheerfully old. The answer, he realized, was, in fact, no – not a bloody bit of it. Reflections didn't make him look old. Being old made him look old. That was the curt message. Hazel would have put him right on this, like a smack in the chops. The reflection couldn't create age, simply told him about it: the reflection, as in some famous tales, was the messenger, not the message. At home, when shaving or about to, he had taught himself more or less automatically to set his features into the shape he knew was guaranteed to provide an OK and non-geriatric mirror version.

Here, in a shop, or on his way to enter a shop, he found himself suddenly confronted by a version of his face he wasn't used to or ready for or kindly towards. As a result, he had to suffer. Or he would have had to suffer, if he didn't get rid pronto of that dreary reflection by his smartly applied forearm curtain. Pensioners ought to be officially and forcefully warned about the possibility of brutal, demoralizing shocks cruelly built in to big shops. Supermarkets were not super for every age group.

Continuing this spell of miserable self-examination, he considered for a moment the private investigator notion. Yes, notion, nothing more than that. Hell, would you commission work from someone looking as old and permanently roughed-up as this seeming dead-beat and pleased-about-it in these nuisance mirrors? The seedy, past-it figure was him: mirror, mirror on the wall, or in the shopfront display, who's the worst prospect of them all as sleuth? I am.

He found now that supermarkets, with their damned shelves stuffed to the ceiling, gave him acutely depressing problems. The lanes of goods they formed provided wonderful, infuriating cover for anyone wanting to lose a tail. You could be apparently loitering in one of these shelf areas inches away from the target in the next one and not know it because of the impenetrable wall of cereal packets or tinned soups or cut-price underwear.

Normally, when Harpur did his weekly or twice-weekly stock-up mission here, he might fancifully regard the shelf walls as keen to embrace him – like the jacket lining on the wharf body – and present him with some of the fine necessaries he wanted. They told of plenitude. He loved cramming his fridge and freezer. He had people dependent directly on him for good meals – Hazel, Jill, frequently Denise – and it delighted Harpur that he could see to needs so easily and quickly. Family: there was a true flavour of family about this. It would give him real community feeling and dad status to be lined up with his trolley at the check-out. It was how police were supposed to be, wasn't it – not military, not governmental, responsible to the people generally.

It wasn't quite like that today, though. A different kind of reality got its nose in front here. Harpur had been deftly guided into this supermarket and almost immediately lost his man. He quickened his pace to search as many shelf aisles as possible. He felt a moment or two of panic. Did Hazel have it even more correct than he'd thought? He found nobody suiting the description he'd been working from. Of course, his target might have gone immediately out from the shop and on to a bus, leaving Harpur helpless. In the frozen foods area, a customer in jogging gear said cheerfully: 'I hear that merrymaker, Iles, is still with us, Mr Harpur?'

'I'll tell the ACC you were asking after him,' Harpur said. He recognized Intelligent Percy now, his trolley loaded, mainly with stubby bottles of Tia Maria, probably for a full-scale celebration after the mad acquittal.

'Are you still giving Mrs Iles one?' Percy asked amiably. He freed one arm from his trolley and began a back-and-forth, energetic, graphic shunting movement with it. 'She and her husband might be moving away, I hear. That's according to Bernie Chail. You know Bernie, don't you? Well, of course you do, small-time dealer of the stuff. But he has contacts all over the UK and he says up North one of the police outfits is looking for a new chief constable. Mr Iles has apparently shown interest. That's according to Bernie. Iles's missus might not like that – the distance from her extra-marital. I wouldn't be surprised if Mr Iles had that in mind when considering a move.' Harpur had heard nothing so specific as 'the North' about Iles's possible thinking, not even of rumour quality. The news, if it added up to anything at all, must be very fresh. It certainly had not come to Harpur from Iles. That didn't make it impossible, though. Iles felt no obligation to keep Harpur up to date with his own personal plans.

'Or it's possible, isn't it, Mr Harpur, that Iles thinks he's done as much as can be done here and needs new challenges. People of Mr Iles's brand are often on the lookout for fresh challenges. They believe no challenge is too much for them. Des Iles would be like that.' Percy began to move away.

Yes, usually on one of his simple week-by-week routine catering trips, Harpur could smugly enjoy the sight of all the items on show in a supermarket. These laden shelves were life. They were grub, they were convenience, they were comfort, they were nourishment, they were – he liked the word, 'plenitude' – as long as one could pay and Harpur could, naturally. He had an unblemished card. He was a nice and wholesome part of a great juicy, capitalist, commercial process that kept the world and the world's banks turning. He was a vital element in this city's fine steadiness and peace.

But, as he was discovering in today's difficult game, all

those lavish, very desirable goods on the shelves were an obstructive fucking pest. They formed an alliance of barriers that stopped him seeing who was in the adjoining lane, someone possibly waiting to nip out when it might be safe, maybe into another hide-away part of the shop, or through the supermarket's front door, free to wander or go to ground.

Harpur stopped wandering and paused in the cleansing section. He felt a sort of despair, even doom, begin to gnaw at him. The waiting unsettled him. Should he chuck this apparently interminable, useless, unproductive vigil? Vigils required something to be vigilant about. A vigil vigilant about next to nothing amounted to nothing to the power of bugger all. He had made a guess and remained disabled by it. Was the target still in that adjoining lane? Had the target managed an exit for himself? Had the target ever been in the adjoining lane at all? What had made Harpur so sure? Did he have evidence? No, he didn't – though most of his life had been about thoroughly collecting evidence. Why didn't he stick with that? All he knew for certain was that the target was not in the same aisle as he was, or not at present. Should he stay put then and simply wait for him to turn up? Would Fate be decent and civil towards him? Nothing that had happened so far suggested yes. But Fate didn't operate to a set pattern.

So as to look like a genuine customer today, he had put a few items from the shelves into his trolley. Frustration at the hapless delay almost forced him at one point to grab some of these off-the-shelf commodities and fling them at the walls of goods. Wasn't he too important and big-time to be in this sick situation? But although he had a bottle of Spruce Up! pink kitchen cleanser ready to be hurled at a shelf section full of similar aids and ripe for destruction, he somehow held back.

And that 'somehow' could, in fact, bring Harpur some high-grade luck. Intelligent Percy, his trolley clinking joyfully ahead of him, reappeared in what Harpur had come to think of as his own terrain. Percy must have gone to other regions of the shop after their conversation but had finished his collecting and would be on his way to the check-out now. He seemed to have a few more bottles of Tia Maria, forming a dodgy,

impressive tower, plus some champagne magnums. Harpur
lowered his arm. He didn't hurl the kitchen fluid.

Intelligent paused alongside Harpur and said: 'That university bird also still tending to your special, imperative needs?'
he asked. 'And she looks after less glamorous requirements
as well, does she – you stock, she cooks what you deliver. Mr
Harpur is well known for the glorious charms of his kitchen,
especially when the student is in it.'

'I'd like you to do me a favour, Percy,' Harpur replied.

Did that sound contemptibly pleaful? Yes, it did, but he
needed help.

'Anything for you, Mr Harpur, it goes without saying. I
don't hold grudges. Some do, especially when a court is
involved.'

Perce had a wonderfully genial and welcoming face, and
this was a considerable aid with his main occupation, street
robberies and muggings. It gave him a rapport with jurors,
too, men as well as women. He probably knew that Harpur
saw through Intelligence's off-the-peg sweet temperament, but
still almost always treated him with the same warmth and
brotherliness as he did for everyone else. Harpur thought he
looked absolutely right behind this mound of rich, glinting
liqueurs and wine.

Harpur put his cleanser back on the shelf. 'Thanks, Perce.'
Harpur gave a quick description of his target: male, alone,
average physique, white, fair hair, leather jacket, carrying a
bag. 'Seen anyone like that?' Harpur asked.

'Shoplifter? Honestly? Shall I do a bit of a dragnet for you?
Have you got a campaign on? Bit low grade for your rank,
isn't it? Aren't you interested in that undoubtedly deceased
at the sand and gravel wharf? Is it a Des Iles idea? I've heard
that dead man at the docks described as a harbinger. Don't
harbingers turn you on, Mr Harpur? Doesn't he harbinge a
troublesome, future-worrying prospect? Does that scare Ilesy?
Can't he see a role in it for him? Or are you expecting
a special large-scale thieving attack today?'

Often, there were police calls to a supermarket because a
customer, or customers, had piled up a trolley or trolleys,
with expensive drink and were making a dash with this booty

for the door, not the pay check-out. Percy didn't look at all as if he had this in mind. He radiated entitlement and had none of the twitchiness; that would almost certainly come if he were planning a trolley-sprint to an illegal exit. Today, Perce was at one with the local community, not robbing it for now but doing what the community did when it came to the supermarket – innocently and neatly choosing goods and ostentatiously paying for them, just as Harpur would when on a normal shopping trip. Perhaps Percy even had a prized discount card to set against heavy purchases. To most people, Intelligent would look just right for a supermarket regular, his hair still reasonably thick, expertly cut and shaped into small, tidy furrows behind the ears like mid-management or an auctioneer.

At the end of the shelf section they shared, Percy, about to start his search on Harpur's behalf, paused and gave him a happy smile and small wave with his right hand where he stood with the trolleys, Percy's own and Harpur's. 'Look after mine while I do a bit of scouring of the scene for you,' Percy said. 'Don't be afraid that you'll look like an alco with all that booze. Tia Maria is a very classy drink, too expensive for most, perfect after a fine dinner. Ask Mr Iles. It's the kind of thing he'd know.'

For a second it seemed that he would step back to Harpur, maybe give him further encouraging, strengthening words. But, no, Intelligent resumed his own trek and went out of sight around the end of the division. His walk was sturdy and reassuring, the walk of someone who believed he had just recruited a detective chief superintendent. Harpur felt interesting. It was an improvement on those fucking mirror insults he'd been getting from himself. Hazel might have told him he was not, in fact, interesting, but Hazel wasn't here.

In a little while Percy reappeared again, though not where Harpur expected. The supermarket had large windows on the western side overlooking the car park. Harpur was shocked to see Percy there, slinking quickly among parked vehicles. Watching him at work Harpur found it easy to imagine how he would be able to slip away after a mugging. He had time, though, to glance back through the glass at Harpur and give another of those mini hand signals. This wasn't just a chummy gesture. Harpur thought it meant, 'Watch this, Mr Harpur.'

He observed that ahead of Percy was Harpur's target. Percy kept a sensible distance behind him. You'd think he'd been trained. He was in and out among the parked vehicles but never lost contact.

Harpur saw a woman in the front of a parked blue Fiat. She seemed restless in the driving seat. Possibly she had seen through a wing mirror the target approaching. She opened the car door, stepped out and walked around to the rear of the Fiat as the original target drew nearer. She'd be in her early twenties, wearing a cerise blouse and dark jeans. The target took a parcel of some sort from inside his bag and handed it over. She put it in the boot, then locked it tight.

Harpur moved forward urgently with the two trolleys, one in each hand, Percy's crammed with booze, the other almost empty. He was making for a couple of the supermarket's wide delivery doors, thirty yards or so away. Perhaps the target and Percy had used these to exit. Now, Harpur wanted to get to them while the transfer of the package was still under way. As Harpur awkwardly progressed, he must have fouled a security beam – or, more likely, one of the trolleys must have – and alarms began to scream all over the shop. They were set to indicate when a trolley, or trolleys, were used as part of one of those attempted multi-bottle getaways. Percy and the target had no trolley or trolleys with them, so might have been able to sneak clear, unchallenged. Harpur, though, did have a trolley, trolleys. Two. One of them, or both, did the nuisance damage. How would a private dick deal with this?

For a couple of seconds, Percy looked confused and mentally off-balance. But then, Intelligent's intelligence kicked in and, gazing at Harpur, he obviously understood what was happening. To the swarming Security people it would look as if Harpur were making a break-out with a stolen, rich cache of bottles. Harpur still had a protecting hand on Percy's full trolley.

'I warned you against looking guilty, didn't I, Mr Harpur?' Intelligent elbowed Harpur gently away from the trolley and broke Harpur's grip on it. Intelligent replaced it with his own.

He did some minor shakes of the head as he looked at his trolley load, as if checking everything was present.

Intelligent spoke to what Harpur assumed to be leader of the supermarket's Security: 'This is Detective Chief Superintendent Colin Harpur. But I expect you know that – have often seen him interviewed on TV News about local crime.'

'Of course.' Security was a short, plump, cheery-looking woman in her forties.

'I asked Mr Harpur to take care of my trolley for a brief while so I could have a quick smoke outside,' Intelligent said. 'And I did tell him there might be an embarrassing moment or two, though I didn't visualize this one. Like a good guardian he followed me out and obviously set off an alarm. It's a false alarm I'm afraid. We're very sorry to have troubled the Security department, aren't we, Mr Harpur? There's no thieving to detect and stop. Chief superintendents don't go in for that kind of trivial crime, do they, Mr Harpur? They leave it for someone like me – someone very like me.'

A few customers had gathered around, interested in the apparent kerfuffle. There were some questions from Security handled very professionally by Intelligent Percy. Things settled back to the normal, Percy pushing his drink collection. When Harpur glanced about, he saw that his target had disappeared in the melee.

NINE

O nce . . . well, possibly twice, but definitely not more than twice, Harpur had heard the name Chail – Bernie Chail – come up in conversation between Denise and Hazel at home in Arthur Street. The number of times it had happened was important for Harpur to feel more or less sure of. Hazel was his daughter, Denise his steady girlfriend. They were not Jack Lamb. That is, they were not informants, and he had no wish for them, or either of them, to leak confidential material to him. To overhear something once, or, at a stretch, twice could have been – was – an accident. The name might be part of the normal social atmosphere at the university where Denise was a student, and at Hazel's school. It didn't prove Denise and Hazel were on something because they knew and used the name of a pusher. Harpur wouldn't regard it as much of his business if they were – especially not Denise: she was old enough to make choices. He was one of her choices so he'd be biased. But, although Harpur would never ask either of them for special, inside information or other names, he had heard their mention of Chail and the tone in which it was spoken. This tone was one of awe and fear. It seemed to tell him that Chail had big status among middling dealers in this domain or adjoining.

Of course, Harpur had most probably heard of Chail before this, but not as someone so notable. Francis Garland was working on a list of people from that level in the trade as suspects in the wharf murder. None of them would be at the grade of wealth enjoyed by Ralph Ember or Mansel Shale. That was the point: those with moderately successful businesses would have an envious eye on those like Ember and Shale, longing to displace them.

In the interests of continuing peace, non-violence and stability, Harpur thought he'd better focus a bit of concentration on Chail – treat him as something more than one of the pack, the peloton. After that mad episode at the supermarket, he'd decided to abandon any hope of turning himself into a private investigator on retirement. Hazel had it right. He lacked the kind of mental structure required for that kind of stop-start, harum-scarum type of career.

Following the supermarket disaster, Harpur felt he could not allow things to end like that – no end at all, really – and he had walked at slow pace towards the car-park entrance and the road beyond. He hoped that the unhurried pace would help him gaze around and possibly spot the target. No luck. He went out into the surrounding housing estate and continued the same leisurely bit of touring. Children on scooters tried to knock him over. In a while he realized he was walking in a circle: he was back in the supermarket car park. He went to join up with his Ford and found what looked to him very much like the target sitting behind the driving wheel. He touched a button and the driver's window dropped.

'Hello there, Mr Harpur. I thought I'd find you here.' He smiled an exceptionally delighted smile, a cheery smile.

'Did I leave the keys?' Harpur said.

'Keys are history, surely. I did want a word. A long time since I messed about with keys, yours or anyone's.'

'Which?' Harpur replied.

'Which what? Mr Harpur?'

'Which word, the word you want?' Harpur replied.

'I felt this was a setting that couldn't be bettered. I had it in mind from five minutes after I woke up this morning.'

'A lot of people get ideas then.'

'Make the most of them I say,' he replied.

'To do with what?'

'With Mansel Shale.'

'Manse? What to do with him?'

'Anxiety, deep anxiety. People walking about here in their usual manner wouldn't spot that he could be suffering the way he is. Manse doesn't do display. That's not his style. What's going on inside is something else though.'

'I've known Manse a long while,' Harpur replied.

'Of course you have. He wouldn't want me to approach you in this matter otherwise.'

'He's had some very bad moments,' Harpur said.

'I take it you know his business colleague.'

'Ember?'

'Exactly. Likewise you'll know Ember's home – the mansion, Low Pastures.'

'Where he lives with wife and two children.'

'Plus?'

'There are more? Some I don't know about?' Harpur said.

'There's a gateway.'

'Naturally. This is a big property and all the features of a big and important estate are present including a fine pair of gates on to the road.'

'Including also a couple of guardians lurking, never far from those gates.'

'Oh, yes a defence patrol.'

'Who ordered this defence patrol?'

'It's routine for some vulnerable properties.'

'Mr Iles ordered it, didn't he? Has Manse got one? No. Why not?' He changed tone. 'You'll ask what is this to do with the trick I've just run involving your car. It's a wheeze we used to pull when I was a teenager running with a bit of a gang in Lewisham, southeast London: get into an owner's car and wait for him/her to come back to it. Then we'd give a lovely, warm greeting. What this said was, we could have driven off in this car leaving the motorist bereft. We were creating trust. We were announcing that the car's defences, such as lockable doors, were no bloody good at all because a kid troupe could open it up and then hang about in totally relaxed style in the happy vehicle to demonstrate that it might not, in fact, have still been here, but it *was* still here, and there perhaps ought to be a good fee for those who'd ensured it would be just where it was left by the usual driver in case that next time the space might be occupied by a different car, not this previous owner's at all, because that one had been driven away to somewhere confidential where it could be traded in for much more than the car-park fee originally available from me and associates with no hassle. Manse used to be part of the Lewisham federation when he was younger and living in London. He was – is – keen to follow that model now because, as he sees it, both undertakings concerned the same theme – trust. Manse rang and wanted someone to do a bit of detailed research on Iles. He didn't think it could be done direct, but sideways on, as it were.'

'By me you mean?'

'By you or someone like you. Manse has your Arthur Street address, of course. I could get on your tail from there. You must be kept in the dark about the Iles aspect – kept especially from you because, obviously, Iles is a close colleague of yours, perhaps a friend as well as a work-mate. But Manse needs to know he can be trusted. He asks why doesn't Iles give him guardians like those at the gates of Low Pastures. Does he want Ralph Ember kept in danger, exposed, vulnerable for some dirty plan of Mr Iles. I was central to Manse's scheme for protecting himself – for finding out all I could about Iles but secretly. But then there's all that terrible, flagrant foolishness at the supermarket today. These are the kind of circumstances that created huge uncertainty and farce. I can't work in such conditions. But then, all that astonishing stuff today in the supermarket – I decided it wasn't something I could keep hidden. Everything had changed. There was a woman involved and another woman in a Fiat and delivery of a parcel. I felt it was crazy not to talk to you about it before I spoke to Manse.'

TEN

Hazel was right: Harpur needed to feel he had a strong, solid, stoutly constructed organization behind him to help deal with any crisis. He realized this probably meant Iles. An alliance with someone like Intelligent Percy wouldn't do. That was only a temporary fluke, leading nowhere except to mess up. The bulky titles of his and Iles's jobs – detective chief superintendent, assistant chief constable (Operations) – proved and endorsed the existence of a big and bonny system. Harpur went to see Iles. Harpur couldn't have said why moments like this came occasionally to him. Harpur wished they did it oftener.

'I've been thinking of Chail, sir,' Harpur said.

'Bernie?'

'The name's around quite a bit,' Harpur replied.

'I wondered when you'd get to him,' Iles said.

'It's only lately that he's come to seem a bit of a worry.'

'Why is that, Col?'

'Because of you.'

'Me?'

'If you went,' Harpur said. 'Went to another post.'

'How would that affect Chail?'

'You maintain a certain climate here, sir. That would be up for grabs.'

'A climate up for grabs,' Iles replied. 'Have they heard about this at the Met Office?'

'We don't want it to happen,' Harpur said.

'Which "we" don't want it to happen?'

'Us,' Harpur said.

'Which us?'

'Me. Everyone in the city who's sane,' Harpur said.

'They love me, do they, Col?'

'Who?'

'Everyone in the city who's sane,' Iles replied.

'Most likely,' Harpur said.

'You?' Iles said.

'I'm glad you've fixed on Chail as of possible significance. But I should have realized, sir, that you'd spot something special there, something not necessarily good.'

They were in Iles's suite again, the ACC pacing-pausing-pacing, Harpur on a straight-backed office chair. He said: 'As you will have discovered, Chail and a few other small-timers are readying themselves and their flunkies for major trouble when (if) you go to another Force.'

Iles said: 'Yes.' He paused. He was in uniform. He took his cap from a shelf. 'He'll be at home this afternoon. I know his timetable and his address, of course.'

'Of course,' Harpur said. 'It's outside our territory.'

'Certainly. That's what makes him interesting for us, isn't it, Col?'

'Is it?'

'He's looking our way enviously,' Iles said.

'I was expecting that I'd have to tell *you* that, sir, not the other way around,' Harpur said.

'Naturally you were,' Iles said. 'Most people find themselves tagging along behind me.' He drove. 'Chail was on the edge of that little war at the Ferris wheel fairground, wasn't he? But he got away with it.'

Chail lived in Verson Close, a small group of modern detached houses not far from a roundabout on to the motorway.

'Bernie! Here's a treat,' Iles said when Chail opened the door. 'I hope that doesn't sound over-familiar, but I feel I know you already, know you well. And I'm sure my pal and colleague here, Col Harpur, would say the same – a fine treat, wouldn't you echo that, Col?'

Harpur didn't answer.

Iles said: 'These visits out of the blue, so bracing and warm for all concerned.'

'Well, possibly,' Chail said.

'I don't blame you for the caution, not a bit,' Iles said, 'and neither would Col, I'm sure, would you, Col, oh definitely he wouldn't. Some, in fact, call Harpur Cautious Col.'

Chail took them into a conservatory built on to the back of the house in the rear garden.

'All the glass!' Iles said. 'How I approve. It shows neighbours there is nothing secret or sinister about this call, despite my uniform.'

There was a baby in a beige carrycot on a kitchen table at the far end of the conservatory. Iles had a smile already in place when they entered the house with Chail. He extended this when he saw the cot. He walked a few steps so he could look down at the child who seemed to be asleep. Harpur wondered whether Iles's research took in the baby. The big smile seemed to have an element of surprise in it. He took off his cap and carried out a sweeping bow with the hat in his right hand. Iles said: 'I wouldn't say it was entirely Harpur's idea to make this visit. I think I can claim some part of the credit, but shall we say the preponderant factor was the Col Harpur factor. He's not one to demand special recognition of his skills and achievements, but fortunately I am here to see that he gets what he's unquestionably due.'

'We hear plenty about possible aims and ambitions, Bernie.'

'Harpur can be blunt,' Iles said.

The baby had a body-length shiver.

'Blunt and impatient,' Iles said. 'Some would call it rude. They can't see that behind a roughish exterior he means well. Perhaps he doesn't. It's not something you can ask him face-to-face, is it? "Do you mean well?" Most probably he'd reply, "What are the options?"'

The conservatory had several blue leather easy chairs and Harpur and Chail had already sat down. Iles came now and took the one next to Chail.

'His mind – Harpur's – ranges quite a bit,' Iles said. 'You'd be amazed, Bernie. It's the kind of mind we'd all do best to keep on the safe side of if that safe side is available. The baby in its cot would almost certainly grasp instinctively the unique aura Harpur brought to any situation. That enormous shiver just now was probably meant for him, but my aura overrode it. This kind of mistake can happen with auras. We're talking subconscious matters here, of course: babies can't be aware of such mystical areas. But their bodies and nervous system respond to the unknowable. Harpur's mind tells him – tells me too – that you would be a total, unreclaimed fucking idiot to think you have a hope of getting your palsied self a comfy billet now or in the future on our blessed ground. We thought we'd drop in to mention this to you.'

'Thank you,' Chail replied. He was tall, thin, bony fingered, dark, retreating hair cut short.

'Why, now here's Mama,' Iles said. 'As expected.'

A woman of about Chail's age – mid-thirties – amiable looking, nicely balanced, fine complexion, came into the conservatory and went at once to look at the baby who was still asleep.

'What do you mean "as expected"?' Chail said.

'Oh, yes, spot on,' Iles said.

'Have you been tracking us?' Chail said.

'Splendid to meet you,' Iles said.

'Mr Iles and Mr Harpur want a discussion re their domain and what is impending,' Chail said.

'We don't know what's impending,' Iles said.

'You probably know more than the rest of us,' Chail said.

'I can see you're concerned mainly with the baby, Mrs Chail,' Iles said. 'That could not be more natural.'

'I'll make some tea for our guests, Maud,' Chail said.

'I'd prefer you didn't,' Maud Chail said.

'Oh?' Iles said.

'Why not, Maud?' Chail said.

'I see no reason to entertain them or to give any sign of civility in their direction, such as tea,' she replied.

'I don't think I've met anyone called Maud before,' Iles said. He did a triumphant double-fisted handshake above his head, like a boxer in the ring congratulating himself on a win. He switched to a different sport. 'There's a Maud associated with a quite famous poet, W.B. Yeats, who wrote about a rugby star who kept dropping passes, "the centre cannot hold".'

'Who the hell do they think they are, the pair of them, barging unannounced into our property?' Maud said.

'A good question,' Iles replied. 'Who do we think we are, Col? But there's a clue, I've called you Col.'

'It's whom,' Harpur said.

'What?' Iles said.

'It's whom do we think we are?' Harpur said. Or was it?

'Ah! Have you been going to English language lessons again, Harpur? Hopeless.'

'I don't like to think of you two being in the same room as Egret the babe,' she said.

'If you don't like to think of it, don't think of it,' Iles said. 'I can tell you this, Maud, that although you have in coarse terms declined to make Harpur tea, he will not bear an eternal grudge. He is well known in the profession for taking hatred based on tea, or the absence of tea, as of passing significance only. If you offered him tea now, despite your previous rejection of such an offer, he would most probably tell you to shove your tea up your arse, but this is unlikely to have been accompanied by a physical onslaught, even though Harpur can on occasions throw a nice punch. Egret is a charming and useful name because, as you probably know, there is a little egret, very suitable for a babe and then the ordinary egret as the child grows.'

'One of you did the job on the wharf victim, if you ask me,' Maud said.

'Nobody did ask you,' Iles said.

'Or you're covering for the one who did,' she said. 'You don't like someone acting alone. You don't feel you have total control. Or then again, there's those small-timers in the trade. You look after one or more of them, do you? Eliminate the solo quester who's trying to maximize his take by acting alone. Competition for one or more of your favourites? Bang, he's gone.'

'It was "Bang, bang",' Iles said.

The baby began to cry and snuffle noisily. Iles went to the cot and fanned Egret with his uniform cap. In a while the din faded. Then Egret began to chuckle. 'I told him a filthy joke,' Iles said. 'Is it a him? Egrets come in both types or there wouldn't be any. If this is a she, I'll need to use an even filthier joke.'

There was a kitchen door joining the conservatory to the house. Iles went through it now and for a few minutes Harpur lost sight of him. 'We came to give a reminder about the paradox,' Harpur said. 'It's a word someone hatched in our territory. It means it's nuts to try a takeover of a blissful, tranquil patch like ours, because it could only be done by destruction of the bliss and tranquillity, so attractive in the first place.'

'Do I hear the corny paradox song?' Iles said. He came back from the kitchen carrying a silver tray with four mugs of tea, milk in a small jug and sugar on it. 'Total and infinite bollocks, paradox. Think of Germany – smashed up thoroughly in the war, back to loveliness and calm a year or two after.'

He went to each of them with the tray and gave them their tea with milk and/or sugar additions when required.

'I had a look around the rest of the ground floor, and then upstairs. Very nice and tidy, clean and decorated for the most part. We can't have everything, can we? Col's got a brilliant tolerance towards dirt. This property, Bernard: we see a lot of its type, don't we, Harpur, whereas Col himself is quite satisfied with a terraced relic in Arthur Street?'

'We're really here to tell you to forget about any advance to new, enhanced circumstances,' Harpur said.

'I found no firearms upstairs or down, but there were at least three locked safes and I could only open two of them – fall-back cash and office papers,' Iles said.

'Like the rest of us, sir, you lose some finger dexterity through age,' Harpur said.

'It's been a treat this visit and your delightfully sincere chin-waggery, Bernard,' Iles said.

'We gave this warning well back, didn't we – a call at The Monty then,' Harpur said. 'No change yet. No change ever if we manage matters right.'

'Harpur often speaks admiringly of that cosy late-night get-together,' Iles said.

'Do we give a fuck?' Maud said.

'Harpur doesn't answer a rhetorical question for every Tom, Dick, Harry and Maud,' Iles said.

ELEVEN

Work on the extension to Low Pastures wasn't quite finished, but Ralph had ordered the display cabinets of china to be put in place. He would fetch a couple of bedroom chairs and liked to sit with Margaret in the new room for a serious rest period now and then. That phrase 'new room' amused her. She said it was what the Methodists in history called their very plain chapels, to distinguish them from the more ornate buildings of the Church of England. This kind of simplicity pleased Margaret. She hated any sign of prettifying. He believed she felt almost as pleased with these interludes as he did, although she could be a bit sharp about all the developments occasionally. That's how Margaret was and he'd put up with it. This sort of waspishness seemed to keep her going.

As a matter of fact, her type of directness was in operation this evening. There was a softer side, but it did no harm. Ralph thought this tidy little gallery was the kind of place where a man ought to sit appreciatively with his wife at well-earned good moments in their marriage. He believed these were not scarce.

Ralph's fondness for china and porcelain was instinctive, though in these last few years he had read up quite a bit about some of the famous houses, as they were termed, such as Sèvres, Nantgarw and Dresden. Margaret had known some of this background already in that way of hers, and Ralph felt a duty to catch up. He didn't mind her being a fraction or two ahead of him in some aspects of life, but nothing vast or humiliating.

This evening they were talking about education for their children. Ralph had wondered if it would be a good idea – no, a suitable, obligatory, almost no-choice idea – an idea to send them away as boarders to a famous, high-achievers' school. He had the name of one near Brighton on the south coast,

Roedean. In his view, it was an inevitable decision for a family like his, owners of a fine property now, once home for the lord lieutenant of the county or, at a different period, the Spanish consul. The right schooling was a matter of proper status, part of the overall social rating. Most probably the school had a scarf with its colours on so in the winter at least anyone in the know could tell if a child had been to Roedean and was certain to have good table manners.

'You'd be welcome to view my Nantgarws.' Ralph could imagine himself framing this offer to someone he'd met at a Roedean parents' occasion. It would be naff to make the invitation more gushing than in the simple, unextravagant 'welcome', because people likely to be at such a function didn't normally talk oily and high-falutin' stuff such as 'extremely welcome' or 'more welcome than I can possibly say'. And obviously – very obviously – if you were welcoming somebody it couldn't be more than you could say, because you were saying it.

Ralph would like this type of select visitor to see not just the Nantgarws and so on, but Low Pastures itself. The guest would note, for instance, the paddocks where his daughters practised for gymkhanas and that kind of thing: riding was probably familiar to many Roedean parents. Ralph was very eager to extend his business to people of this wealth and class. Newspaper articles said there were increasing openings in that area. There were more rich folk about, getting richer.

There might be a safety element, too, in shifting the children's education if the trouble he sensed was on the way here, or was here already. At present, Ralph's daughters attended a local fee-paying school, but clearly it was nowhere near the quality of somewhere like Roedean. People already knew Ralph's children and their family were of a distinguished category. He was looking for the next step, and the next step might have to be a steep one – Roedean or similar. Ralph would have liked to get some tattoos but he considered it would be unwise except for foreigners.

In the new china gallery this evening, he stood up and walked around the cabinets slowly, checking the presentation was as good as it could be. Ralph had come to suspect that

very much in life was about presentation. He wanted to be
sure in case a visitor failed to get the full glory of his collection right away. It had to be strongly effective, or he and Low
Pastures would not win the sort of brilliant hoist to their
reputation he wanted. Such recognition didn't just show up
by nature. It had to be worked for. And it had to be worked
for particularly when he felt things generally had begun to
look very insecure and shaky. No, that was not true. Others
might not notice any insecurity and/or shakiness, but Ralph
was exceptionally sensitive to signs in the atmosphere of
approaching perils.

'So tranquil and soothing at present,' Margaret said, gazing
through one of the extension's windows at a few of the Low
Pastures acres.

'How do you mean "soothing"?'

'Soothing after that ludicrous business with the ladder. And
what is it with Detective Chief Superintendent Harpur in
general?' Margaret said.

'In what way?' Ralph replied.

'Things around here are all tranquil and, yes, "soothing",
but it's rather frail, isn't it, Ralph? I think of Harpur up the
ladder, poking about unbidden in this extension. No real
account from him about why he was there in the middle of
the night, and what he was looking for.'

'It's all fixed now,' Ralph said.

'He's important, isn't he?'

'Up to a point,' Ember said.

'He's a crucial part of the tranquillity and peace in this city
– he and Iles. They're like a team. Take one away and look
out for trouble. Balance disrupted. Are there rumours about
Iles looking for a post elsewhere? Apparently, there's a great
deal of job swapping among chief constables. It's called
"churning".'

'He's still with us. He hasn't been churned.'

'And there's the matter of Harpur, a chief superintendent
up the night-time ladder. It's . . . well, disturbing.'

'That was very feasible. They could have heard about the
building work and realized it might provide an extra way in.'

'OK, OK, you can say, Ralph, that I also was up a ladder

here in the middle of the night, firing a gun, shouting a crazy word to all the world.

'But when I started it was because I feared we had burglars. Kidnappers? I felt I might need a gun, and I knew where you kept yours, very unused but there, easily available and loaded. None of that was true about Harpur. Is he gone slightly stressed? Has that death at the sand and gravel wharf knocked him a bit haywire? And now another rumour the children have heard about: this time, Harpur involved in a strung-out, comical, very degrading incident at the supermarket. Is chaos clawing its way in?' she said.

'A mistake, or series of mistakes, sparking each other off,' Ralph said. 'Farcical. It's a tale started by a dubious citizen familiar to everyone, police included, known as Intelligent Percy. There's often a weird sort of matiness between major detectives and big-time crooks. So much of their lives overlap. It's unavoidable.'

'All the same,' she said, 'it shakes the civic structure a bit, doesn't it?'

'Does it?' He was unhappy about the way the talk had moved. He tried to bring it back to their original topic – education of the children. He felt Margaret didn't altogether appreciate how important this topic was. They'd be out of the area and free from danger if they boarded. His thinking wasn't totally unrelated to that bigger subject, though. Did the dead man at the wharf foretell something dark and bad and threatening for the city, for the region, in fact?

Of course, quite a long way back, Ralph had hinted to Margaret there might be an end to the lovely calm and tranquillity of the city. She'd been unimpressed then, reduced it all to one very pretty term, 'paradox'. But events like the ladder episode and the supermarket absurdity had obviously made that casualness impossible now for her. Slipshod – that's how Margaret's good mind would judge it. And there'd been that worrying warning visit to the club by Iles and Harpur. Although Margaret had told him she enjoyed these relaxed sessions in the Low Pastures extension, they were not glossy and promising enough to 'soothe'.

Ralph saw that he'd need to provide something more,

something stronger, something decisive, perhaps something warlike, tearaway and thuggish. He went back to sit with Margaret again. She turned her head and smiled. It was a warm, comforting smile, but he thought there was an element of pity in it, too, and he fiercely resented that.

TWELVE

Harpur had a landline call at home from Jack Lamb, rare these days, which, on the whole, Harpur considered a good thing, though there had been a time when such exchanges were frequent. His daughter, Hazel, answered the phone first this evening before handing over the receiver. Her chit-chat with Jack was warm and light-hearted, including some big laughs from Hazel. Her attitude towards him had changed lately, become benign.

Lamb was far and away Harpur's best informant – possibly the best informant of any detective anywhere in the world – and Hazel and her sister, Jill used to despise that relationship. They called it by all the standard terms of contempt, such as stool pigeon, grass, telltale-tit, traitor. They wouldn't actually use any of these terms of disgust face-to-face or on the phone, but they directed a deep coldness at him. Harpur knew Jack was bound to sense it, and would be hurt.

But, recently, they seemed to have softened. Harpur felt grateful. It was as if the girls had come to recognize that a number of the most sickening and destructive crimes could be uncovered and stopped only with inside information. Inside information often added up to authentic evidence, and courts demanded authentic evidence. It could be very difficult to come by, and it was getting more difficult. Secret whispers from someone like Jack was one way of getting it, not that there were many, if any, in Jack's class.

Tip-offs could not be used in a court because – because they were only tip-offs. Jack would never go into a witness box. Jack provided something to start an investigation with, generally, Harpur. Iles's policy of lasting serenity in the city at any cost meant that toleration of the drugs trade brought major crime steeply, reassuringly, down: informants didn't have a lot to inform about. And so Harpur's daughters could at present regard Jack as quite near to an ordinary and amiable businessman who helped their dad sometimes. He responded in a similarly close tone, actually seemed to feel some fatherly affection. This was not at all like the worrying fondness Iles sometimes showed towards Hazel, though Harpur thought that seemed to have abated, thank God.

From the period when Jack's service as a Harpur informant was active more often, and when Jack was therefore in plenty of danger if identified, they employed a series of secret, rotating meeting spots. These had been a strong habit and Jack, a bit sentimentally, liked to continue using them now, even though occasions were fewer. Tonight, at his suggestion, they rendez-voused on a hillock at the rural edge of the city. In World War Two anti-aircraft batteries had been stationed here to blast at incoming enemy bombers. The artillery was gone, of course, but the concrete emplacement and rails for the ammunition trucks remained.

Jack wasn't the only one who favoured this location: back-seat adulterous lovers in their cars also lingered. And, as for Harpur, he enjoyed the contact with local history. It gave depth and helped him prize the city laid out beneath them, made it absolutely worth saving. In his head he would try to imitate the engine noise of a gaggle of Heinkels, on their crusade at night to drop high explosives and incendiaries, but this he'd stifle and overlay with the roar and clatter from the imagined hit-back barrage. It made Harpur feel positive. Naturally the city would have been blacked out during a raid. Now, though, the streetlights formed a bright, clear pattern, north–south, east–west. Harpur took a delight in that spectacle, and so did Jack.

'I don't like to think of them ashamed,' Jack said. 'We have to end that. Why I phoned.'

'Ashamed? Who?' Harpur asked. They were sitting in his car.

'Hazel. Jill, too.'

'Ashamed? Why?' Harpur replied, though he knew what Jack meant. It wouldn't be the informing. They seemed to accept that now as a painful need. No, Jack meant events, recent events.

'They're fine kids,' he said.

'Of course,' Harpur said.

'I expect they get some joshing and spite at school,' Jack said.

'Joshing? Spite?'

'Children can be damn cruel,' Jack replied.

'Mine cope, I think,' Harpur said.

'Oh, yes,' Jack said. 'But it's the combination of things – the sort of amassing of your antics lately. Other kids will mercilessly mock, and they especially like mocking the police.'

'Amassing? Antics?'

'Piling up.'

'Of what?' Harpur said.

'Behaviour. Yes, that's what I'd call it,' Jack said.

'Call what?'

'The behaviour,' Jack said.

'But what behaviour?'

'The rumour around. Or rumours, rather.'

'Which rumours?' Harpur said, knowing which.

'Luckily, I've got something – brought something tonight – that might help us deal with it.'

'With what?'

'I hear of some craziness at the supermarket,' Jack said. 'You and Intelligent Percy.' Jack's voice hardened. It was as if he thought Harpur had formed a new link. Jealousy? Not sexual, professional. 'Bottles, Intelligence said.'

'It was just a fluke and accident, a mishmash,' Harpur replied.

'Bad for your . . . well, profile. Unstable, Col. That's how it seems. Idiotic. Your image compromised. We have to guard what we've got. This could damage all of us. And then, previously, you on a ladder in the night at Ralph's place. Apparently one of the cow herds from Apsley Farm was biking up early to help at a calf birth, hears a commotion at Low Pastures and cycles over for a quiet, clandestine look, sees you up a ladder in conversation with Mrs Ember, recognizes you from TV News. More rumour? Probably not. We don't need events of that kind involving you, Colin. It suggests to me a breakdown of control, and would to anyone reasonable. Carelessness.'

'Yes, all a mishmash,' Harpur said.

Jack was about 6 feet 5 and 250 pounds. Even seated, slightly crouched behind the windscreen in near darkness, he looked formidable. Harpur always listened respectfully to him. It was usually worthwhile. To be accused of 'behaviour' by someone like Jack carried quite a punch. He and Harpur were both fans of control. Their alliance wouldn't function without it. There was worry as well as condemnation in Jack's voice when he referred to Harpur's recent exploits. This was a lot of worry when it came from someone built like Jack and with a brain. He would often assume briefly unusual, flamboyant clothes – an odd taste for someone who believed so strongly in staying if possible unobserved, but today he was in a black wool/cotton-mix topcoat and black jumper, not at all flashy. Harpur wasn't sure what this meant – either it was too important an occasion or not important at all.

'Mrs Ember is very sensible,' Harpur said.

'It's been a mistake, Col,' Jack replied.

'What has?'

'To let these meetings lapse. There have been consequences,' Jack said.

'Which?'

'Frequently these last few days I think of the dead man at the wharf.'

'We have an ID for him,' Harpur said.

'I'm sure, but have you any idea why he got hit?'

'Chief Inspector Francis Garland is working on that – in cooperation with the Met. Your dead man is from London. He's nobody much,' Harpur replied.

'Right. He's nobody much, hardly anything at all. He got in the way of someone much, much bigger.'

'That's an ID we haven't got,' Harpur said.

'The wharf lad had gone buccaneer, as they call it in the trade. Maverick. No discipline. So, Mr Sand and Gravel Wharf had to go: two bullets in the back of the head. It happens in these gangs – someone thinks he or she is not going to get a big enough slice of takings and so sets up a personal business instead – or tries to. That kind of thing can't be tolerated by the rest of the gang, though. They fear the competition.'

'Two rounds, yes, I thought so,' Harpur said.

'His girlfriend, Rebecca Something, comes looking for vengeance and there's probably money involved, of course.'

'I met Rebecca,' Harpur said.

'I know you did, and it led to the supermarket, didn't it?'

'A tailing job, and I started there. It was to please my daughters. They want to see if I could survive as a private detective. Hazel doubts it.'

'Yes, I know that, too,' Jack said. 'I think they'd heard about you and the ladder and wanted to make you stop fooling around uselessly.'

'Mr Iles was – is – worried about Ralph's safety. He'd put a couple of our protection people at the entrance to Low Pastures. That doesn't please everybody. Some suspect a plot. Many are surprised at how caring Mr Iles can be.' Harpur put a nice helping of ooze into these concluding words.

'Yes? I gather, Colin, a woman arrived in a blue Fiat, a woman in her twenties. Did you know her?'

'No, not at all. Still don't.'

'You're sure?'

'Never seen her before. She did what she had to and then immediately drove off.'

'Where women are concerned I, and possibly others, think of you as a trifle ungovernable, especially women in their twenties and driving a chic car.'

'It wasn't so very chic,' Harpur said.

'But she was in her twenties.'

'This was Thursday a.m.?' Jack said.

'Yes,' Harpur replied.

'Was the meeting prearranged?'

'Not as far as I was concerned. How could it be?'

'Phone? E-mail?'

'I've told you, Jack, I didn't know her. Still don't,' Harpur said.

'No, I can believe that, Col. I was only testing.'

'Thanks.'

'My information is that you seemed surprised, bewildered, to find the Fiat there,' Jack said.

'Your information? Where does it come from, Jack?'

'A contact who recognized you. Many would. You're on TV, and your picture in the local press now and then.'

'Someone who knew you'd be interested because of your link with me? It's worrying, Jack.'

Lamb put a hand out in front of him, his left hand, then put the right hand on top of it. He dislodged his left hand and put this on top of the right and then dislodged the right and put this on top of the left. It was as though he was building a wall, or a prosecution case, brick by brick, fact by fact, each layer dependent on the one preceding it. He wanted to show Harpur how he reached his conclusions. Gradual. Methodical. Systematic. Reliable.

'Promising?' Jack said.

'How do you mean, promising?'

'Nice looking, well made, that sort of thing?'

'It wasn't what this was about,' Harpur said.

'What was it about?' Jack asked.

'Not at all clear,' Harpur replied.

'She didn't remain in the Fiat, did she?' Jack said.

'No.'

'I understand she got out of the car and went to the boot, which she opened.'

'Correct.'

'Did she need a key?'

'I think so. I can't be sure. It wasn't easy for me to see. There was quite a little crowd gathered around because of an incident involving trolleys. I didn't have an uninterrupted view of things.'

'Yes, you had two trolleys, didn't you? Not usual in a supermarket.'

'Intelligent Percy had asked me to look after his.'

'Why couldn't he look after it himself? This was a trolley full of hooch, wasn't it?'

'He was doing something for me and wanted to be inconspicuous, unhindered and very mobile,' Harpur said.

'Doing what?' Jack said.

It seemed absurd to Harpur to be explaining these footling details on a site where the defence of the realm had been fought out, full scale, eighty-odd years ago. 'I wanted him to make a search.'

'A search who for?' Jack said.

'Well, the man who must have had a rendezvous with the Fiat woman,' Harpur replied. 'I know more about him now.'

'There was a parcel, wasn't there?' Jack said.

'She received it,' Harpur said. 'That would seem to be why she was there.'

'How did you know that would happen?'

'I didn't. It was Intelligent who'd found the searcher, and the searcher who met up with the Fiat woman.'

'The parcel?' Jack said.

'I didn't know what it was and don't know now.'

'What shape? What size?' Jack asked.

'A box, brown-paper-covered, sealed with sticky tape.'

'What kind of box?' Jack asked.

'Like a shoebox.'

'An adult shoebox?' Jack asked.

'I don't swear to a shoebox. It wasn't that sort of situation,' Harpur said.

'Which sort?' Jack asked.

'Not the kind of situation where I would have expected to find a shoebox being handed over – this was a supermarket. It's the wrong sort of setting for that. But if it was a shoebox, yes, an adult's shoebox.'

Of course, Harpur could see which way the questions were going. He had asked himself the same sort, though not taking things as far as the adult/child difference.

'This is where the key, or no key, becomes important,' Jack said. 'Doesn't it?'

'Right,' Harpur replied.

'This is not a big parcel, is it, Colin, whether adult or child shoe size? It's the kind of parcel that most of us would probably leave in the car, not bother with a probably lockable boot for it. That would suggest, wouldn't it, Colin, that this parcel has some special unique quality that needs to be out of sight and adequately looked after: for instance, put in a locked car boot and conveyed immediately to a specific recipient. I'm talking about a gun, aren't I, Col? Something valuable, rare, dangerous, possibly incriminating, for potentially deathly use, and up to now untraceable and therefore worth all the precautions requiring, as an essential, a key.'

Harpur felt their roles had been reversed from the usual: Jack was supplying the questions and Harpur the answers, the information, except that there wasn't much of that.

'Was anything spoken between the two when searcher handed over the parcel?' Jack asked. 'This was a resounding, culminating moment, after all. We might expect it to be marked by some strong greeting, perhaps even an identity password.'

'For part of that time she had her back to me,' Harpur said. 'I couldn't tell whether either of them said anything during those few minutes. And then when she closed and locked the boot, nothing was said. I'd certainly have remembered if there had been.'

'A smile, a nod, by either party?' Jack said.

'Not that I recall.'

'That would suggest an agreed prearrangement, wouldn't it, Colin, even rehearsed?'

'Possibly.'

'These two might be simply carriers, briefed to do this fairly basic job, not knowing its significance or context,' Jack said.

'Could be. But do you think its purpose was supply of a pistol?'

'I can't imagine what else,' Jack replied.

'Wads of money? Sensitive documents, rare brandy, a brilliant, fragile ornament, a pair of specially crafted adult shoes? Those two, probably in a hired car for this particular task and ordered to carry it out by their boss,' Harpur said. 'Gangland boss?' He made it sound melodramatic.

'Mock not, Col. I don't think you know what murk is around us now. What would *you*, for your part, say was in the parcel? Aren't you interested? By the way, are you still comforting his wife, Col?'

'As to the ladder, I wanted to take a look at where the Embers might be vulnerable,' Harpur sort of replied, 'At the extension join I mean. Just routine safeguarding, Jack.'

'I hear Ralph's wife had a pistol under the bowler hat she was wearing,' Jack replied.

'I wanted a chat about prospects,' Harpur said.

'I don't suppose I'm the first to ask why that had to be done then and there. The rumours are plentiful,' Jack said. 'All of them added together, "amassed", makes this situation look weak, unhinged, precarious. Perhaps out of the mishmash comes the decision by the superleader type in London that now's the time to take advantage of the weaknesses here and move on the sweet, quiet, cash-juicy patch – the Iles, Harpur patch. Our decent, wholesome, un-blood-soaked streets. Is it the due moment? That's why I said I've brought something, Col.'

He put his hand under his lapel. The movement – its slow, determined pace – set up in Harpur strong memories of something very similar, but for a moment he couldn't recall what it was. He found he was quizzing himself, the way he just now had been quizzing Jack for clarity.

Then his recollection became plain, obvious: he had made this kind of reaching out when he searched the dead man at the wharf, feeling for a pistol in his shoulder holster. Forewarned by this recollection, he speeded up the movement and put his hand over Jack's, stopping any progress. In some ways it looked like a comradely gesture, even a loving gesture, but no, a barrier.

'I can't take a gun from you, Jack.'

'Why not?'

'If I needed one, there's the police armoury.'

'You do need one,' Jack replied. He spoke as though the long gap since their last meeting had made Harpur naïve and ignorant.

'You're involved in a dicey situation without realizing it, Col. It's not official business, so no HQ entitlement to use of a gun.' He paused, grew sombre. 'Tell me, do you think we can win?'

'We? Which we? Win what?' Harpur said.

'Am I wrong to say "we", like you and I are . . . are, well, a unit. You, a braided cap top cop if you ever chose to wear it, me . . . well, something hugely different.'

'Detectives don't wear braided caps,' Harpur said. 'You and I simply look after each other.'

'In its way it's noble, isn't it?'

'What is?'

'The Iles notion,' Jack said.

'Which? Mr Iles has quite a few of those.'

And then the self-questioning that had badgered Harpur a little while ago came back and started on him again. Might they be right about his dodgy, unworldly 'behaviour' and disorderliness? Harpur asked – asked himself; had he lost some of his vision, a vision that had often enabled him to see through, grapple with, think out, the problems that life, the job and his children flung at him, and instead, had seen him drafted into a handful of farcical episodes: up a night-time ladder or starting a supermarket security clanging crisis.

Never mind about imitation Nazi plane engines decades ago. How about now? That was the sort of thing Jack and Hazel and Jill required him to deal with, and, presumably, the Apsley Farm maternity assistant, and Intelligent Percy. Harpur decided that in case they were correct and he'd drifted into slackness, he'd better try some changes. He relaxed his hand on top of Lamb's. Jack nodded, as if aware of the crucial new Harpur thinking, and resumed the approach towards what Harpur saw now was a Smith & Wesson .38 pistol.

'Here,' Jack said, smiling benignly as though in congratulation. Harpur thought a gift tag, 'Best wishes from Jack, Col,' wouldn't have been totally mad.

Jack passed the gun to Harpur. 'Untraceable,' Jack said. 'I've seen to that. If there's difficulty at any time, just discard. It won't come back to me.'

'What sort of difficulty were you thinking of, Jack?'

'Incursors.'

'Which?' Harpur said.

'There are people looking for new territory, aren't there, Col? This city is new territory for them. They would destroy what they hope to gain – idiots. But they would also destroy our happiness and sweet stability. They have to be negatived.'

Harpur put the pistol into his pocket. 'Yes, that could be called a difficulty.'

THIRTEEN

It shook Harpur to find that the gun did what Jack had obviously expected it to do. No – that wasn't quite it, not so simple. It wasn't just a matter of gun as gun but gun hard against his body in his pocket, the two sensations linked, of course. They seemed to reciprocate, and bring support for each other.

So far the gun hadn't actually done anything he knew of, though: anything notable, such as shooting somebody. In fact, Jack had more or less said it was unused, so far. The lines of the gun were certainly beautiful They bucked up his morale, made him feel substantial, bold, unfragile, definitely not the kind of operator who'd fall into the massive stupidities of that small-hours ladder incident; or the vast clumsiness of the supermarket fuck-up.

Of course, this wasn't the first time he'd suffered regrets for those daft episodes, but today, apparently because of the gun, he could dismiss them from his conscience, at least temporarily. Was this the kind of thing the famous actor, Charlton Heston, felt when he spoke so powerfully in favour of a gun for every family? Harpur longed to find something good and helpful in those wonky adventures.

For instance, what exactly happened at the supermarket? Was there anything he could learn from it? Was there anything a would-be private detective might learn from it? Among all the explanatory and probing words that erupted when Security arrived at the pair of trolleys, were there any that might help Harpur find out more about the tailee? He'd never managed to get a full picture of that ghastly, quaint sequence. Perhaps he'd shut his eyes and mind to it because these facts were so uncomfortable. But, detectives – very senior detectives – didn't shut their eyes and minds to avoid uncongenial facts. Their job was to expose uncongenial facts.

So, what were these facts? He knew from things a couple

of the Security people had said that the alarm had been set off by him and his little wheeled convoy when they crossed an anti-thieving spot or line; and he thought he recalled a burst of loud shouting, which would be from one of the Security unit. They had a uniform, didn't they? Tan-coloured with a blue and red stripe? He remembered that much. There were four or five in the posse, he reckoned, possibly three women, two men, one of the men in charge of the shouting – perhaps experienced in that skill after previous crises. He was a small distance behind the others, eking out the big, necessary breaths needed for his yells.

'Stop, stop, Tia Maria looters. Stop, I say.' He obviously had splendid eyesight: he could identify the stacked bottles and wanted to specify exactly which looters he had in mind today, Tia Maria lucidly and correctly nominated. Maybe he'd needed on a previous chase to bellow the name of a different expensive drink – say, brandy, Pernod, whisky.

Harpur's memory gave him many tiny glimpses of what had occurred, but they didn't join to make an understandable, graphic picture. He saw in recollection Intelligent Percy's hand move his – Harpur's – gently off the laden Tia Maria trolley and replace it warm-heartedly with his, Percy's own, so that Harpur wouldn't seem to be criminally in charge of the alcohol. Gallant. Tactical. But it was OK for Percy, because in another of his flashbacks Harpur heard and saw him produce with his free hand from his back pocket a hefty roll of fifty-pound notes. 'Naturally, I've brought this adequate wedge of currency to pay at the check-out for the drink,' Intelligent said. 'I was having a wander pre this. I think wandering in a supermarket is permissible, isn't it?' he had asked one of the Security team in a slab of banter.

Harpur remembered that a small, curious, excited crowd of shoppers had trickled out through the delivery doors to spectate this confrontation between the Security squad, Intelligent and the target figure. Percy had done some earnest, cooling talk. His spiel had gone something like this: 'But, surely, some of you Security recognize Mr Harpur, a very major detective. Ask yourselves, do, is he the kind of lawless bozo who would try to get away free with an Everest of after-dinner plonk? Can you imagine what his boss, Assistant Chief Constable Desmond Iles, would think of that, how he would react to that? No, you assuredly cannot because it would never, could never happen.'

At some point during this forceful appeal to reason by Intelligent, Harpur had realized that he had lost sight of his target among the security folk and the nosy swarm of onlookers. Harpur had taken a lot of harsh questioning from Security, but gradually the tone of it had lightened, mainly because of Intelligent Percy's strongly respectful words about Harpur's identity. Two of the security force seemed to recognize him after this testimonial, most likely from those TV appearances by Harpur in crime news reports.

Eventually, there had been outright laughter as details of the situation became plainer and absurd. 'A detective chief super with a cart-load of swag!' 'Oh dear, dear, piles of Tia Maria.' But when Harpur tried to spot his target in the chuckling crowd and beyond, he failed. The target obviously knew how to dodge out of this kind of very convenient buffoonery. He'd let Harpur find him in the car park eventually.

Harpur thought now that he could somehow keep his mind in reminiscence function, clear and poised, to make sense of the whole situation. This was quite an achievement after recalling the disastrous culmination of events in the supermarket. Harpur sensed that Rebecca must have travelled to this city to check what was happening in the case of her murdered friend, Lawrence, at the wharf. Perhaps the target had come from London on a similar mission, but also to size up the Harpur and Iles realm. Harpur guessed he must have had a whisper about where she was staying – there'd been plenty of gossip in pubs and restaurants following the local murder. He could get in behind to tail her. It might have turned out absolutely neatly, but it had turned out anything but. Harpur felt he had learned quite a bit, though: there were going to be recurring episodes like this recent one as criminal firms jostled for control of this vastly profitable new space – a lot of criminals, a lot of the dangerous jostling. Where Mansel Shale, the target's former London colleague, fitted into this was anyone's guess. The target had implied they were friends, that he cared about Shale's well-being, but how long for?

Harpur learned as well that some aspects of an investigation might never become clear; this seemed particularly so about the baffling minor travels of the shoebox parcel. Failure to understand every detail about a case wasn't unique to Harpur. Every detective was sometimes defeated. Harpur would occasionally ask Iles for help if he was stuck, but this didn't seem like the right kind of problem to involve him in now. Harpur wondered whether a well-established private investigator might manage to sort it out. He wasn't that.

Harpur let his mind slip back again. He'd kept tabs on Intelligent after the trouble, and had got himself and his trolley close to Percy as they made for the check-out. The Security troupe had accompanied them. There were occasional outbreaks of applause from customers and staff as the Target, Intelligent and Harpur passed.

He'd had enough of this craziness and wanted some neutral topic to discuss with Intelligent. He could do without any more hilarity about the alarm fiasco. He'd nodded towards the bottles and remembered pretty well all the conversation about them, it was so interesting.

'Where will the celebration party be, Perce?' Harpur had asked. 'Ralph Ember's club, The Monty?'

Percy had unleashed a very thorough guffaw. 'That dump? Hardly! My mother would never allow it. She likes to maintain what she regards as a decent social standard. There'll be her judges, fashion goddesses, lordlings, bishops, brigadiers among the guests. She wouldn't want them obliged to mix with lowlife. She'll run the do at her place, of course, the Bay Penthouse, music from Toejam, a top-class pop group. Acquittals deserve the full treatment in her view. I'd give you an invitation – honestly, Mr Harpur,' Percy had said, 'but I know the bouncers would be told to keep out anyone . . . well . . . anyone not what she'd refer to as "perfectable".'

'Ember is working devotedly to bring the club up to very select standard,' Harpur said.

'She's heard about that,' Percy had replied. 'Mother thinks

it will never blossom. "Impossible". She likes to keep her eye on things generally from her gorgeous nest in the Bay.'

'Ember will stick at it,' Harpur said.

'Of course, you've got a soft spot for Ralphy, haven't you, Mr Harpur?' Intelligent said.

'He doesn't like being called Ralphy,' Harpur had replied.

'Too bad.'

'Soft spot?' Harpur said.

'The word's around.'

'Which word?' Harpur said.

'Up a ladder at God knows what time of night at Ralph's place, making sure the precious china's OK. Mother thinks Ralph is trying to do too much in his lust to get pukka – extending Low Pastures, extra prettifying for The Monty. She believes there are going to be immense changes – real changes,' Perce had said.

'What changes?' Harpur asked.

'Not the kind of piffling alterations Ralph is messing about with. This will be a true shake-up. Did you catch what he said?'

'What who said?'

'Your target, as you call him.'

'There was too much talk and confusion. I missed some of it,' Harpur had replied.

'He said, "I'll be back. You've only seen the start of it at the sand and gravel wharf." I hope I'm around to help you again, Mr Harpur.'

Intelligent had become very solemn then. He'd said his mother would think of the knockabout in the supermarket as part of a much bigger scene.

Perce had said: 'There was some sort of deal done, yes? I sense delivery of something very significant. A gun? Possibly a gun supplied by one of the small drugs firms. Or *for* one of the small drugs firms. Someone was waiting for it over a period of days, but then this sudden siren shambles, everything goes missing. Anarchy. It still prevails.'

'It does, Perce,' Harpur had replied. There hadn't been much else to say.

FOURTEEN

Ralph took Mansel Shale on a drive through the city, and then out across the two counties nearby to the north and northeast. Manse wasn't good at visualizing from words. He wanted to see the actual. And Ralph *wanted* him to see the actual. By 'the actual', Ralph meant he would show Mansel the site of some terrible recent violence in these neighbouring areas. Why? That was an easy one; because it was the kind of terrible violence that might come next to this home patch – Ralph's and all those enjoying that home patch with Ralph, such as Manse, Margaret, Harpur, Iles, the whole very special local population. It had to be stopped before it arrived.

Ralph felt very strongly that he himself could deal with the words-and-ideas side of matters. This was not Shale's sort of thing at all. It would be a kind of cruelty to require that from him. But he had other fine assets, not just business skills but life and death. He'd had some rough experience of these, and knew how to apply what he'd learned.

The car trip today was Ralph's first move in his plan to break away from all the hesitations and indecisiveness that had held him back lately. Held him back from what? He recognized this was a fair question, but he had a fair and formidable answer. He thought those who feared that an onslaught of some sort was very possibly due – was very *likely* due – were right, and this was the time to put an end to it before it started. Ralph saw this as an important, perhaps vital, journey with Manse, and it had taken him a while to decide how to run it. Was this another deliberate, evasive delay? But he couldn't allow that. He had made himself immediately consider the options: should he handle it alone or organize some help? Well, everyone had heard about what happened when Harpur tried to act solo. So Ralph had resolved to look for some assistance.

Look where? Should he do a trawl for a suitable, professional gunman? The idea hadn't appealed to Ralph. He felt that for a job of this kind he needed someone he knew and whose actions and reactions he could count on. And there would be security worries: he didn't want the project discussed by hired partners or pals. That's how dangerous rumour was born and how whispers thrived.

Therefore, he had chosen Manse, someone he'd known for years and whom he more or less trusted and who most likely more or less trusted him. Theirs was a marvellously effective partnership.

Ralph lifted a hand from the steering wheel and pointed towards a fairground, with a Ferris wheel in operation ahead on the other side of the road.

'That's it, Manse.'

'Is that it?'

'That's it. There was battling for best part of an hour before enough armed police turned up.'

'An hour? "Three dead, one amputation".'

'Three dead?'

'Three dead and a leg,' Ralph said. 'Not our ground but very close. It could come our way soon. We've got to prevent that.'

'I think I've seen him around.'

'Who?'

'The one-leg.' Mansel said: 'In a way he was lucky, wasn't he, Ralph?'

'Which way?'

'A hospital near, able to do that job,' Manse said. 'Think, if it was Antarctica, Ralph.

'This is the kind of sickening violence they want to bring to our lovely city. They were running around with their weaponry and daggers, firing from behind the Speak-Your-Weight machine, coconut shies, Electronic Ambush stalls, fortune-telling tents.'

'What's that?'

'What?'

'Electronic Ambush.'

'Oh, yes. Fairground people have to keep up with the state of the new technology, Manse.'

'All this – the way you explain things, Ralph, is a great help to me. I've been very anxious these last weeks. I could tell something was wrong, or would be in a minute or two. Ember gets protection at home and I don't. Why? I asked a London mate from the old days to get me a gun – just in case. I was going to pick it up by what you could call "special delivery" in a supermarket car park, and then it was all ruined – the careful arrangements – when Harpur, the detective chief, very nearly messed everything up. But no, he didn't, I got the pistol and had the feeling it might be needed. It's made me a bit edgy. You calm me down, Ralph.'

Ember didn't fancy an analysis of Shale's anxiety. Ralph had word of the supermarket trouble but hadn't realized Manse might be part of it. Ralph saw a parking space, pulled into it and stopped. He brought from his pocket a piece of white card. It had on it what looked like a line drawing, or basic map of a ground floor somewhere. He showed it to Manse.

'Ah, yes,' Shale said.

'You see what it is?' Ralph said.

'Ah, yes,' Mansel said.

'You sure?'

'Ah, yes,' Mansel said.

'Here's the Ferris wheel,' Ralph said, pointing to the sketch.

'Ah, yes,' Mansel replied.

'And here's the Electronic Ambush and the coconut shies,' Ralph said.

'Anyone could see them,' Mansel said. 'This is graphic.'

'What does it tell us, Manse?'

'We can learn a lot in that sketch,' Mansel said. 'Grand.'

'I'd meant to put arrows on, but forgot.'

'Yes, arrows might be useful, but it does the job just as it is. Definitely,' Manse replied. 'It's possible to get through the situation without arrows. I wouldn't have known you'd forgotten the arrows unless you'd told me. I can take arrows or leave them alone.'

'The arrows would show the stage-by-stage direction of the attack, using the various tents, stalls and huts as firing points or cover. These arrows would have indicated progress, relentless, quick.'

'Ah, yes,' Mansel said. 'I'll admit the arrows would have been a plus, but they are not indispensable.'

'And this tells us, I believe, that they can and will scheme. They've been successful so far by scheming to bring enemies down – and perhaps we are now that enemy, and they have evolved an impressive way of doing it,' Ralph said. 'It makes sense, doesn't it, Manse, to think that if the rumours are right and there are outfits waiting to take over our area, it would be a mob – or mobs – close to ours geographically. They will have heard of the grand trade done here and favourable Ilesian philosophy like sunshine for the Whitsun Treat.'

'Mr Iles knows religion,' Shale said.

'What?'

'Religion. That Whitsun Treat, Whitsun's religious, isn't it?'

Ember started the car and they drove away.

'I'm going to keep that in my mind,' Mansel said.

Ralph had, in fact, brought him out to see something he could keep in his mind – the slaughter site.

'Good, Manse,' Ralph said.

'Yes, Whitsun.'

'Whitsun?' Ember said.

'Sunshine and the Whitsun Treat.'

This was the thing about Mansel: if you were discussing an idea or ideas with him, such as Iles's views on policing, Manse would always fail to get the main point or points. There were times, of course, when he wasn't wrong, and you had to hope you'd catch him at one of his clear, important moments. He could be formidable, even totally devastating, then. This was not one of those moments.

FIFTEEN

Of course, informants had informants. No informant could be expected to see everything, hear everything, himself/herself.

Jack Lamb was in touch with Harpur unusually soon after the gun meeting. Jack had had a whisper. It was a whisper he reckoned would interest Colin Harpur, and after so long he also obviously reckoned he knew what should interest Harpur. On this he was right. Like most careers, informing operated in stages: there was a beginning, a middle stretch, a conclusion when the information reached whom it was intended for.

It was Jill who answered the phone this time.

'Have you got a bag of sparkling disclosures for Daddy?' she asked. Harpur picked up the extension.

'He might tell you,' Jack said.

'No, he won't and you know it,' Jill replied.

'True, he can be a bit unhelpful,' Jack said. 'It's his training.'

'Can't you show him how to shed some of that? We're his flesh and blood, aren't we? Doesn't that bring privilege? OK it would be limited privilege, but privilege just the same.'

'Not really my job, Jill. He goes his own way.'

'Isn't some of that against the rules?' Jill said.

'He doesn't make a habit of it,' Jack replied.

'We talk over these little parleys.'

'Who do?'

'Hazel and I. But we realize all the time that these calls could be only a fraction of your contacts with Dad. We are shut out.'

'Are you asking me whether this is the case?' Jack said.

'You spotted that, did you?' Jill said. 'You've got a brain.'

'Thank you, Jill.'

'Dad wouldn't be snitching to you if you didn't, would he?'

'I think that will be enough now,' Harpur said.

'Goodbye Jack,' Jill said. Harpur heard her put the phone down. He had to check that.

There was reassuring silence for a while and then Jack said: 'Jill sees the difficulties.'

'She has a brain.'

'I thought that was me,' Jack replied.

'We're waiting for you to come up to the mark,' Harpur said.

'Ember,' Jack replied. 'I've got something on him, though I'm not sure what.'

'Ralph?'

'Ralph and Mansel Shale,' Jack said.

'Exemplary pair,' Harpur said.

'Out together.'

'That would be unusual, Jack.'

'Out together to some purpose,' Jack replied.

'What purpose?' Harpur said.

'Unknown,' Jack said. 'So far.'

'A pressing purpose?' Harpur said.

'Unknown.'

'But you wouldn't be ringing if you didn't consider it pressing, would you?'

'Think of the North Road,' Jack said.

'Well, yes, I know the North Road,' Harpur said.

'A trusted source of mine, driving out that way, sees a parked Renault, and recognizes the two men in it. But the source is travelling at a fair speed – this, though, not unduly fast, I don't like contact with speed fools – so can't be sure and drives on, then turns for a repeat viewing and confirms. As sources go, this one is very reliable. The two men recognized are Ralph Ember and Mansel Shale. They're reasonably familiar to the source from a career in the kind of work handled over the years. I was glad the source made the two drive-pasts and saw that nothing had changed on the second. It's an encouragement.'

'It sounds to me as if Ember and Manse were viewing something,' Harpur said.

'You've got a brain, Col,' Jack said. 'First sight of them by accident or fluke, a bit of roadside fleeting interest, then second, more considerable and deliberate visit in case the two were still there, which they were. So the question is, what is it they're looking at?'

'Not easy to answer,' Harpur said. 'They do nothing except record impressions in their minds. We can't get in there.'

'Maybe not, but I've been out to the parking space,' Jack said.

'That was thoughtful of you,' Harpur replied.

'Routine. Jill wouldn't like to hear of a job only half-done.'

Harpur said: 'She's very influential.'

'It's an uninterrupted view of the Lixxt fairground and the Ferris wheel. That's what seemed to grab their mature attention, my source said.'

'I hope you pay a respectable whack for such outstanding service.'

'Col, please don't talk about money for this kind of work,' Jack said. 'We agreed a long time ago that it would be off-limits.'

Occasionally Jack could turn pious and prissy like that. Perhaps the good conversation he'd had with Hazel had brought this on today. She and Jill used to be scathing about the Jack–Harpur link. The work 'snitching' that Jill had used just now made Harpur wonder whether she was undergoing a return to contempt for Jack and informants, and for those who dealt with informants, like himself.

'Sorry, Jack,' Harpur said.

'Judas has a lot to answer for.'

'Your source, Jack?'

'What?'

'Obviously very thorough.'

'They're like that, aren't they?'

'Who?'

'Women in this game.'

'I don't know any woman in this game,' Harpur said, 'until now.'

'Yes, she's reliable.'

'About what age?' Harpur said.

'Thirty-seven, four months, no, five.'

'As sources go, it sounds as if she's quite close,' Harpur said.

'She knows the kind of thing I like,' Jack said.

'Yes, I expect so.'

'I mean the kind of work.'

'Of course,' Harpur stated. 'Does she know about me?'

'She knows that someone titanic is not far off. She knows he has to be satisfied.'

'Does she know how well she does that?'

'She gets no details about you and she has a degree in "discretion", Starred First, anyway.'

Harpur said: 'Name?'

'Daisy.'

'Does your source provide for anyone else?'

'Provide?' Jack said.

'But I suppose sources don't source about their own sources,' Harpur said.

'No, we don't.'

'Daisy is a source, Jack, and you source to me,' Harpur said.

'That's exceptional,' Jack replied.

'Good,' Harpur said. 'More than good – wonderful, Jack. When Daisy comes back on the second peep, they hadn't moved: is that right?'

'They were like before. As far as Daisy could tell,' Jack said.

'Looking in the same direction?'

'Right.'

'So what is it? What are they looking at for such a while? You've been out there, haven't you, and you'd get some idea of their view?'

'Well, of course,' Jack said. 'It would have been sloppy not to. The Ferris wheel made it easy – conspicuous. Ralph and Manse seemed to be focused hard on the fairground.'

Harpur wished Hazel and Jill had been able to watch how the fragments gradually joined in an investigation because of the strong and steady contribution of informants. They'd be pleased, wouldn't they, that clever, devoted people like Daisy and Jack were happy to work with their dad?

'This fairground was a battle site, wasn't it, Col?'

'Bad. Deaths, surgery.'

'But not in your area.'

'Neighbourly. The past. But these things can come alive again now and then,' Harpur said. 'That's what we wait for – or expect our sources to wait for.'

'Daisy thought from how they were sitting that Ralph Ember might be . . . sort of . . . well, sort of "instructing" was her word . . . instructing Shale in something.'

'How would she judge that?' Harpur said.

'Daisy has opinions. She said their head positions were fixed and their shoulders angled similarly towards the windscreen. No smoking. Possible conversation going on but, if so, talking straight ahead not breaking the gaze towards the fairground. But Daisy was too far away to hear any talk or to lip-read.'

'So, not casual – not just a matiness session or an opportunity for a chat,' Harpur said. 'They are in a settled attitude for at least as long as it takes for Daisy to carry on and reach a turning point, probably in someone's driveway, then come back.'

'I saw where she had most likely done a reversal,' Jack said.

'Of course you did, Jack. We've said it would have been sloppy otherwise,' Harpur said.

'It would all take about three or four minutes,' Jack said, 'the manoeuvring and the actual distance, twice. And maybe they'd been like that for a time before Daisy spotted them, and afterwards.'

'It's strange. These are business associates – very close business associates, with a long history of cooperation, yet they apparently have to meet in a bit of a layby, not in their office or home,' Harpur replied.

'But if they want to share some special view, as we've suggested, Col, they've got to be at the same place and at the same time to see whatever it is they need to see,' Jack said.

'I'm interested in Daisy's word "instructing",' Harpur said. 'Who's doing the instructing, who's getting instructed?'

'Well, Ralph's behind the wheel so I think Daisy assumes it's Ralph's vehicle and that it's his operation.'

'Which is what, Jack?'

'You're the one to answer that, Col. You're the one who might be able to do what you call "getting inside their heads".'

'Perhaps. Not my sort of magic guesswork,' Harpur said.

'Nor mine,' Jack replied.

'Daisy's?' Harpur asked.

'Daisy wondered if Ralph was trying to get Shale back into violence mode in case things become rough by showing him how matters had developed in very adjoining territory not long ago. She thinks Ralph must be turning proactive: that's another of her words. Manse has to live with the memory of his murdered wife and child, doesn't he? Ralph possibly wants to tap into that reservoir of rage by showing him the kind of murderousness that always lies close by. Daisy seems to think Ralph is ready to initiate trouble, not just wait for it to hit him and the rest of us on the Iles–Harpur domain.'

'Feasible,' Harpur said.

'Daisy's always that. She sees Ralph repairing himself by taking Manse as an ally and hopes to prepare him by getting him to think violence – to breathe and believe in violence. He's offering Mansel a share in a major project, but the offer arrives with conditions.'

Hazel came not too soundlessly back into the room and gave Harpur an unforgiving stare for being so long on the landline. There'd been a time when Hazel announced to Harpur: 'This house is a home. It has three occupants – occasionally four – you, me, Jill, Denise, and the occupants have equal rights to any fitments.' This had been said with a level tone, laden with threat.

Jack said: 'What we have to bear in mind, Col, is that Daisy might've been seen during her reconnaissance, especially on the second visit when she must have been driving slowly – sort of loitering – to make such a complete survey possible. She was building a picture of their psychologies from their faces and way of sitting in a car. It can't be rushed. She's on show as much as they are. Daisy is aware of that danger. Likelihood? After all she had noticed them so they might have noticed her. That's what this episode is all about, isn't it?'

'Certainly,' Harpur said.

Hazel did a couple of heavy breaths.

'You have company, Col?' Jack said.

'Hazel's monitoring,' Harpur replied.

'She might have a view on the teasers that are baffling us,' Jack said.

'Yes, she might,' Harpur said. 'But not now.'

'The drawbridge is coming between Jack and you, Dad,' Hazel said.

'Did I hear mention of a drawbridge?' Jack said.

'Yes, and that's as much as you're going to get now, I think,' Hazel said.

'Is Daisy a cracker?' Harpur said.

'Who's Daisy?' Hazel said.

'One of Jack's friends,' Harpur said.

'Dad means big boobs, neat bum,' Hazel said.

'I didn't get all of that,' Jack said.

'If she's something special, she's likely to stand out and get observed, and not just by you,' Harpur said. 'They're focused on the fairground, not girls. She's a workmate of Jack.'

'Oh yes?' Hazel said.

She went and sat in one of the big leather armchairs near a telephone extension but did not lift the receiver. Now and again, Hazel did exercise a fragment of tact and restraint, despite how Harpur worked. Jill might not be the same, though.

SIXTEEN

arpur decided he'd better go out and have a look at this seemingly crucial location on the north, north-eastern road for himself. He was getting information from what certainly felt like perfectly reliable mouthpieces, but they were not mouthpieces that spoke directly to him. The tip-off came by phone from Jack Lamb, Jack had received it from someone called Daisy, unknown to Harpur though, apparently, not to Jack. There was plenty of room for errors in this devious process.

Normally, Harpur would have believed and acted on anything that arrived from Jack Lamb, probably the most gifted and accurate informant anywhere. But his information now was to do with a sort of nothing topic. That is, it speculated that an ordinary bit of roadway might indicate that some big, crooked, violent plan was in formation and likely to destroy the harmony of this region. Harpur also reasoned that there might be an emotional/fleshly connection between Jack and Daisy which could affect the kind of work they produced together. Harpur was ashamed to realize that he had such doubts about Jack, but he had to acknowledge to himself that sometimes they did exist.

He didn't like leaving the non-official gun that Jack Lamb had given him around when he wasn't present, and he put it in the breast pocket of his jacket. He drove out alone in an unmarked squad car to what he thought must be the parking spot. He had no trouble finding it, although there were no parked cars there now, and he could see at once why it must strike the others as significant.

'Hello, Col,' Iles said, pulling the door open as Harpur arrived. Iles put a hand forward and did a feel of Harpur's jacket.

'Ah, gun-up, are you? I expect your dear mother told you never travel without a .38, my beloved boy. Mothers have a

good deal to be said for them, but for God's sake don't bother
to say it, Col, will you? One of our traffic people saw a couple
of cars parked eccentrically not long ago and did a check on
one of the reg numbers. The check showed Ralph Ember's
ownership. The Control Room chief considered I'd be interested and told me. She'll go far. I decided to keep an eye on
this drab piece of ground, carry out an intermittent watch. And
how was it with you, Harpur?'

'What, sir?'

'Why are you out this way?'

'My mother had no views on .38 pistols as far as I can
remember,' Harpur replied.

'Mothers would favour a gun that can nestle snugly in a
pocket of a well-cut jacket, or even in a crying-shame alleged
specimen of tailoring like yours. The fact that I could spot the
gun's neat build can't be blamed on your mother. Irrelevant.'

'Thank you, sir,' Harpur replied. 'I'm sure she would be
very grateful for such tolerance.'

'She would be full of warm memories with you as a child
talking about the grand advantages of the .38 automatic job.'

'These are good recollections,' Harpur said.

'Your mother would be the kind who instantly understood
why her fine boy would be out in this fucking shithole of a
nowheresville today, greeting his assistant chief (Operations).
Specifically me.'

'Thank you, sir.'

'Your superior having given a full and remarkably truthful
explanation of his own presence here expects a basically polite
response from the assistant chief (Operations) who waits,
tolerantly, for a courteous and respectful matching answer.'

'Somebody mentioned it,' Harpur said, 'following noticeably
sharp eye-work.'

'Mentioned what?' Iles said.

'This fucking shithole of a nowheresville,' Harpur said.

'Why did he/she mention this shithole of a nowheresville?'
Iles said.

'Mention to me.'

'Well, it would be to you, wouldn't it, Harpur, being the
kind whose bloody mother puts a pistol in his pocket?'

'It wasn't my mother,' Harpur said. 'It wasn't anyone's mother. A chum.'

'Good,' Iles said. 'I hate hearing of promiscuous mothers. What time would they have for skateboarding?'

'But there's no denying the gun is snug. If my mother had thought much about guns in those days, she would have probably picked a .38 and put it in my breast pocket. However, many a mother might do that for the welfare of their lad.'

'Yes, we must give them credit. There's a move towards larger calibre handguns,' Iles said. 'They're not really suitable for a pocket. Get your mother to write protest mail, Col. Resist, resist. Quite a few mothers about lately, aren't there? Intelligent Percy has a mother, hasn't he?'

'I'll definitely look into all this,' Harpur replied. 'Of itself this place where we find ourselves mysteriously together is of flimsy importance, I believe.'

'Do you, do you? Or is it, as we've already described it, a shithole nowheresville. But perhaps you have more information than me, your assistant chief constable (Operations). It would not be the first time such a disgraceful and mutinous situation has been contrived by you, Col.'

'Mutinous?' This wasn't the term Harpur would have used to describe his attitude to Iles. The word recalled for Harpur a famous film, *Mutiny on the Bounty*, occasionally brought back on one of the movie channels, where the brutal captain played by Charles Laughton is ousted by one of his officers, Fletcher Christian, and set adrift miles from anywhere in a small boat. 'I'll see you hanged, Mr Christian,' the captain says. And so he does.

But Harpur didn't hope to displace or even diminish Iles. Harpur wanted to look after himself and was confronted by someone who wanted to look after *himself* and skilled and ruthless at doing it. Police forces were full of such high-ranking – but not the highest-ranking – officers.

And so, Harpur did what he could – and what he could was plenty; especially how to manipulate the flow of informant information, which was more likely to come his way, rather than Iles's, because the supreme part of Harpur's job was informant material. Harpur had to preserve that kind of

information, if necessary sit on it or hide it. Maybe he let a
little of it emerge occasionally, but it would be rationed: enough
to maintain safety of the informant and, as it happened, prevent
Iles from knowing too much about what was going on, particularly if what was going on looked liable to be crucial to the
advancement of the ACC's career.

Iles was wearing one of his excellent, single-breasted, light-
grey suits and white training shoes with red and blue stripes.
Harpur had on a white shirt, open at the neck, and a lightweight
jacket. They got out of their cars and pace-measured the
parking space together. 'Hey,' a woman called loudly, 'what
are you doing all the time up here exactly?'

'Up where, exactly?' Iles replied.

'Here. Strutting.'

'Strutting? Who?'

'You,' the woman said.

'I don't know how to strut.'

'Don't kid yourself, strutter,' the woman said. 'You'll one
day most likely get an MBE for it.'

'My friend and I like a bit of a stroll,' Iles said. 'Strolling is
very different from strutting. Strolling is leisurely and inoffen-
sive. Strutting is bombastic. You will confirm unhesitatingly this
to the lady, won't you, Col?'

'Unhesitatingly is a very large claim.'

'Strutting,' the woman said. 'In a suit like his, and those
shoes, that's strutting gear. Patriotic training shoes, red, white
and blue. Is this the fucking Olympics? You're a duo.'

'Col has his own style. The rest of us play along willingly,'
Iles said.

'Why?'

'Why what?' Iles said.

'Why willingly,' the woman said.

'Oh yes,' Iles said but didn't answer.

'The other two, recently, sat watching. They stayed in their
cars. It's you and your mate who do the strutting. One of you
is in control,' the woman said. 'You,' she said, pointing at Iles,
'and calling your colleague by different names. I mean such
as "Col". That's officer talk. *You* wouldn't call *him* Col.'

'His name's not Col.'

'What is it?' she said.

'Do you mind being called Col, Col?' Iles said. 'It's nice and easy to say: "There's a call, Col." His mother probably wanted that when they gave him the name. She would be thinking that when he was grown-up, somebody might say to him, when handing the phone over, "It's a call for you, Col. Please take the call, will you Col?" The tone of the person's voice would tell which Col or call was meant, although it would be both.'

'We're talking persistence now,' the woman said.

'Who's persistence?' Iles said.

'People,' the woman said.

'Which?' Iles asked.

'I said which,' the woman replied. 'They were a duo and now you are a duo, strutting. What is it you want?'

'Are we a duo, Col?'

'In a sense, I suppose,' Harpur said. 'At a quick count, there are two of us.'

She was about Harpur's age, dressed in a long woollen skirt and short-sleeved blouson. She seemed to have come out from one of the houses. She stood at the closed front garden gate, looking over it to the street where Harpur and Iles had been walking. They had paused now. Perhaps she'd been doing some observing. It was a street and a district that could profit from more air.

'Col's mother thought quite a bit about .38s as well as names,' Iles said.

'.38s what?' the woman asked.

'Oh, yes,' Iles said. 'When these other duos were around, did you notice what they were especially interested in?'

'I wanted to ask *you* that.'

'I'm not surprised,' Iles said. 'I'm interested in their purpose. One of our purposes is to find what their purpose was. They're a mystery.'

'We don't approve of what's going on,' the woman said. 'We can't relax when there are, or were, strangers lurking.'

'Harpur likes to think he's so affable and hearty that he's not regarded as a stranger,' Iles said.

'Of course he's a fucking stranger,' she replied.

'Who doesn't approve?' Iles said. 'Who doesn't like anyone lurking in the vicinity?'

'People,' she answered.

'Which people?' Iles said.

'People who live here,' the woman said. 'I live here. You can call me Fay, even though you are lurking,' she said.

'You shouldn't be ashamed of where you live,' Iles said. 'People have to make the best of a bad job. Oh, hark at me! That's a kind of sucked-dry commentary on life that idiots and vicars try to shear us up with, Fay. Harpur's mother probably spoke such arsehole wisdom when supplying the .38 into his pocket.'

'What's a .38?' Fay said.

'Oh yes,' Iles said.

'People don't like having other people strutting about where they live,' Fay said. 'They don't know – we don't know – what the outcome will be.'

'Which people?' Iles repeated.

'People such as people we don't know, such as yourselves,' Fay said. 'Why are you here? Do you know the word "casing"?'

'Col might know it. He knows quite a few words,' Iles said.

'Giving the place a once-over for their own reason,' Fay said. 'With an objective?'

'Which objective?' Iles asked.

'That's what I'm trying to find out,' Fay said.

The ill-temper seemed to come at Iles and Harpur in neat, precise helpings, as if it had been packaged and prepared somewhere and placed ready to be flung. The bulk of it was directed towards Iles, and Harpur felt glad of that. It was the sort of thing Iles could officially deal with. People spoke of the shit hitting the fan but in that kind of mess-up, Iles was the fan.

'When I mentioned casing, this is a police word,' Fay said. 'It's to do with drifting around an area, ahead of some dirty business, scrutinizing.'

'Is that why you think Col and I are here?'

'No.'

'Why, then?' Iles said.

'A view?' Fay said.

'Oh,' Iles said. 'A view of what?'

'Across.'

'Across what, where?' Iles said.

'Over to the fairground and the Ferris wheel,' Fay said.

'Col's casing the area for that, do you think? Why?' Iles said.

'You tell me,' Fay said.

'He's a quiet one,' Harpur said. 'Now and then.'

SEVENTEEN

People – especially women – often told Ralph Ember that he looked like the young Charlton Heston. Ralph thought there was something in this. But it was only a matter of physical appearance. Ralph, personally, saw a resemblance between himself and not any actor, however handsome, but a famous character in a theatre play – Hamlet. The thought went considerably deeper than the Chuck Heston comparison. This idea had come very suddenly to Ember, a real shock. He knew where it had begun, though.

As part of his campaign to raise the social stature of himself, Low Pastures, and The Monty, Ralph had begun a mature degree course at the local university. He'd had to suspend it at present because of business pressure, but he'd completed the Foundation Year and meant to resume his studies soon. He had enjoyed the seminars on Shakespeare's plays and particularly *Hamlet*, a drama about the young prince's failure to get his finger out and do something. Of course, if he had done something there would not have been a play, but the lecturers didn't make much of that. What especially fascinated Ralph was the similarity he felt to himself in the unpleasant matter of delay and backing off from action, despite efforts by others to get him going.

There'd been prompts from Margaret, his wife, who seemed to fear that the wonderful calm and safety of the city so far was in danger. Assistant Chief Constable Desmond Iles displayed the same sort of uneasiness. And the dead man at the sand and gravel wharf possibly brought a threatening sign. Ralph hadn't been there at the time, but he'd heard on the gossip network that the stranger involved with Detective Chief Superintendent Harpur and Intelligent Percy at the supermarket had said he'd be coming back, and it wasn't said sweetly. It was a threat. Ralph felt as if the city was tamely lying there, passively, feebly, hopelessly.

Incidentally, Ralph was also told that Intelligent's cow of a mother, rich on stocks-and-shares fraud, had made some slighting, evil comment about The Monty. She was another who probably believed he was pathetically weak. Ralph longed to show this was absurdly wrong.

So, Ralph realized he had to get back to where he once was. In those days it had been more or less routine for him to feel a readiness to kill if required. That 'if required' was important. He had never been merely someone who blasted off at the least provocation, or no provocation at all. He had belonged to a firm that occasionally needed to protect itself and Ralph had gone along with that response. Of course he had. But there had been a change, a development: he was now ready to kill as one of a team, a team of two, and he had to be the main man of that two, leader of that pair. He was the older, the established. He was Ralph Ember and Ralph Ember sky-highed. Ralph Ember showed how to star.

Then there was the matter of flesh, of skin. Oh, yes, this was the crux, very special to Ralph. His idea of leadership and his precedence came with provisos. Shooting wouldn't do. Although he was ready to kill, he was not ready to kill by mere handgun. That didn't seem right to him – unsuitable. It lacked the personal element, was too mechanical, not close enough even if physically close. It missed any – all? – flavour of splendid heroism. Ralph needed this grandeur and flamboyance. Without it, leadership had no significance for him. He demanded the contact. He wanted his supremacy made blatant.

He recognized that death by pistol could have its noble aspects. Defeated generals sometimes shot themselves to preserve honour. But Ralph had no taste for suicide. He didn't want to write off the future, he wanted to dominate the future, the bit of it coming his way: Low Pastures and the extension was the future; the kids' education was the future; a secure, expanding business was his future. He would have liked the school to offer ancient Greek and Latin teaching: that in a special, reverse way was the future.

And he knew he wasn't alone in wanting to drive forward into whatever came next. The future obviously looked good for many in the borough. This is what made it attractive and dangerous. Any menace, he must try to destroy. He didn't expect to bring about such improvement by a bit of pot-shot handgun work. This death required stature and meaning. Detective Chief Superintendent Harpur and Assistant Chief Constable Iles kept things reasonably serene; Harpur with that young, beautiful, bright college student, Iles not so obvious in his private life, but a kind of family man, apparently. Ralph's target might taint this lovely peacefulness and profitability. Ralph would prevent that vandalism if he could.

This starkness in his thinking, this unflinching purpose, came to Ralph with another major condition. It had to. He needed decisive contact with the skin, the flesh of someone. Which someone? Whose skin? Whose flesh? He had to know that. He did know it, didn't he? This was a profound matter of clarity and certainty, surely? Yes, he could rely on that, surely. Surely.

In fact, Ralph was watching someone who might suit now, actually had him physically in view near the Wilson Street corner. If Ralph had been carrying a weapon – if he hadn't made that absolute decision – he could have riddled him right away. The nearness would make this simple and foolproof. It wasn't a matter of 'he thought' he could bring this about and pick the right one from the list of three possibles he'd formulated. Ralph was no longer in that sort of dithering area of doubt and hesitance, was he? Was he? It was not long ago, but not now, was it? Was it?

His present selected target dressed harmless, as it was known. That is, it had been a harmless fashion for people in the drugs trade not long ago, but not long ago was still the past. Too many people had fancied this unobtrusive style and used it. So, the mode had become a sort of label, but a sort of label meaning the opposite of what it was supposed to mean: not at all harmless; instead, devious, smartarse professional, driven by greed beyond the customary even for this brand of commerce.

It was off-the-peg gear, what used to be called a 'sports jacket' and grey flannel trousers, a white button-down collar, done up, and an autumnal-shade tie, a small knot, brown, plus well-polished shoes. The quality of all this was good, perhaps excellent, but wilfully dull and anonymous, It lacked – avoided – the flashiness of some drugs firm chiefs and hadn't yet reached the sort of resounding, big-time reality of Ralph's beautifully solid wealth.

If he hung about certain streets in the centre of town, he might see half a dozen men dressed like this, perhaps see them do some dealings. There could be a couple of women too, but he found them less easy to classify by dress, though there were names around in gossip, or possibly more than gossip. He knew that some women liked to buy their fixes from women. They felt safer. This could be an error.

Ralph saw Bernard Chail manage a couple of quick sales to a mixed trio of teenagers – two male, one girl – and there were lots of smiles and a nice glint of twenties. Ralph could not be sure how Chail ran his business – day and night. Ralph had just watched a deal done in the sunlight of mid-afternoon, speedily, confidently. The apparent smoothness of it might indicate that this was a regular, well-practised service. Might. It could also be a one-off, though, response to a single call, spotted by Ralph only through fluke. Chail was off his proper ground. That could be another explanation for the swiftness.

There were all sorts of variables: availability of supplies, evidence of police interest, enough customer funds and, of course, there'd most probably be potential witnesses about. Not ideal. There was a strange bond he'd noticed between himself and someone like Chail. Ralph didn't much like the idea of doing Bernie – doing anyone, in fact; no, didn't like the idea of doing anyone – in full daylight. He did want a strong personal aspect – the skin element, but not when outsiders might get a privileged look at what was going on. What was going on would be the wipe-out of somebody. Perhaps earlier in his business career, Ralph would have regarded these kinds of objection as footling quibbles. They could still hold him back, though, in this day and age. Pathetic, yes, but absolutely capable of reaching him, hindering him. Since those distant days, he had become Ralph Ember of Low Pastures and The Monty, happy social club, and this required recognition and fitting behaviour, nothing undignified or paltry.

Ralph was watching from behind a couple of parked

builders' lorries, feeding some reconstruction work in a shop opposite. He realized he'd become conspicuous if he stayed there for much longer, though the lorries weren't actually engaged in any of the work at present.

Ralph decided he'd allow himself five more minutes, in case Chail came back. This turned out wise. Chail did come back, and accompanied by someone male, elderly, bearded. They were laughing apparently at something one of them had said. This infuriated Ralph. It seemed so wrong, so blasé for the situation when the safety of a city might be in question. Ralph felt even more determined to see to Chail, a rejoinder to this oafish smugness. He thought they might have a different attitude if they'd known they were observed. He took the laughter as a kind of insult, a disrespect that must be punished. Not to know they had an audience didn't count as an excuse in Ralph's view. The two showed bland arrogance in their giggling. Would they have continued this stupidity if they'd known the significance of these two very useful trucks, useful to Ralph, significance to Ralph?

It struck him that there was something deeply absurd about the situation, something preposterous. The point was, wasn't it, that – until a matter of minutes ago – if he'd thought about lorries at all, it would be as part of the equipment he'd ordered for the improvements at his property, Low Pastures. He had hired lorries and their personnel. In a sense, for now, he was similarly the Wilson Street crew's boss. That was his rank. He was a boss man. But, as things actually were at this moment, he had to cower and scurry and squint around the lorries, scared of being noted, like a piece of slithering low life.

This he was certain didn't mean he took a snobbish down-his-nose attitude to lorries. That would be foolish – the very opposite, in fact, of how things should be, and of how things were. These trucks in this street proved that the town was pushing ahead, was part of general fresh development. There was a bracing, creative feel to the work. These lorries were positive contributors to what might be brilliant improvements to an already fine commercial scene. There were excellent, handsome shopfronts and the intriguing opening to a wide arcade. Ralph was very fond of arcades: stuff on offer from both sides, and all of it in a sheltered, nicely kept setting. Arcades typified the way towns ought to be, in Ralph's opinion – beautiful, thriving, protected. He was ready and eager to provide that protection.

Although this reconstruction and the vehicles had nothing to do with his Chail mission, some of the debris in the lorry nearest him greatly interested Ralph. There were half a dozen old-looking bricks, still cemented together to form a kind of L, maybe part of the upper corner in a room or corridor. The bricks had a faded appearance now because of time and the probable absence of sunlight.

Ralph realized this wouldn't mean a lot for most people, but for him it was the vivid evidence of progress made very wonderfully plain. It told of a structure, of a worn-out structure now; of replacement of the worn-out structure; of the ability to fund replacement; of a new shape and design of somewhere inside.

He would have liked to reach out and give the expended bricks and cement a congratulatory fondle for having done a passable job in there, perhaps for decades. This kind of gesture would make him too obvious, though. But, as an alternative, he could safely speak a tribute. Well, no, not 'speak' exactly. Utter. Only Ralph would hear it, which was not the usual way with tributes. 'Very well done. You helped build a good tradition,' he whispered. He didn't want to be daftly lavish in his praise. After all, he kept in mind that this work poshing-up a shop – even an arcade shop – came a huge way behind the class of his very major improvements at Low Pastures.

Ralph was always conscious of social grades. They had to be respected. He'd discovered there was quite a precedent for this attitude, a famous saying: 'We must have distinctions.' Ralph had begun that mature-student degree course at one of the local universities – the same university as Denise – and remembered these words from a foundation-year history seminar. They'd been used originally by the Emperor Napoleon after the French Revolution and its attempts at '*égalité*' – equality. Ralph totally agreed. He'd put the degree stuff on hold for a year because of business demands, but he recalled plenty from the foundation year and felt a real closeness to the emperor, though he'd accept, of course, that emperors were higher up the scale than he was.

Some of these ranks depended on very fine differences, one just a little above or below another. This would not be the case with these two projects: the Low Pastures level, and the boutique level. Low Pastures was a huge distance in front, but Ralph would still allow the shop operation to get some fraction of his attention. He felt he had a kind of clear duty to offer this. As he saw it, if the proprietor was local, he would certainly have heard of Ralph Ember. There weren't many people in the area who had not heard of Ralph Ember of Low Pastures, and it would probably please the shop owner – if he was inside somewhere – to learn that a citizen of Ralph's business stature should be interesting himself in this very modest, though certainly worthwhile, building project between a greengrocer's and a men's barber's.

Ralph broke off observing Bernie very briefly and smiled chummily across the load of cemented bricks in the lorry at an elderly woman leaving the greengrocer's with a basket of mushrooms, lettuce and runner beans. Ralph would like her to think, 'Good heavens, it's Mr Ember of Low Pastures in person out buying some supplies.' It was only an accident they should meet like that, but then, Ralph thought so much of life happened by chance. He tried to keep himself ready to take any good, unplanned opportunity that came.

'*Bon appétit*,' he said.

'You sodding what?' she replied.

Ralph didn't mind this casual rudeness too much. He saw it as one result of the woman's shock at encountering him in a sneaky situation shaped by rubbish-laden lorries. When she reached home and was chewing the salad, she might recall this incident and regret her impromptu coarseness and hostility. She looked the sort who'd have second thoughts while eating something bland and therapeutic like lettuce.

Ralph switched his gaze back to where Chail and his friend had been when Ralph was distracted by the shopper. They were still loitering there near the entrance to the arcade, perhaps waiting for fresh customers. This spot made a nice assembly point.

Then, though, they seemed abruptly to change. They stepped into the arcade and began to walk quite fast towards Ralph and the lorries. The laughter had gone from their faces. In fact, Ralph could detect no expression there for either of them. They stared blankly ahead to the other end of the arcade. If they continued like this, they would pass very close to Ralph, and he had the feeling that they *would* continue like this. Their behaviour astonished him, baffled him. Bernie was certain to recognize Ralph, even if Bernie's new companion didn't, wasn't perhaps local, and remained unfamiliar with the town's main people such as Ralph Ember. Yet Chail gazed past Ralph, gave him not even a nod. Their faces continued empty.

Ralph came to believe it was an act by these two: they pretended to be unaware. But why would they do that? Ralph suffered a terrible confusion. He had thought he was fooling Bernie by spying on him unobserved. In fact, though, it looked as if Chail had known what was happening. He was fooling Ralph, not vice versa. The life Ralph had built for himself, or thought he had built for himself, was endangered. Bits of it might collapse – might have already begun to collapse. His fond emoting over the broken brickwork suddenly seemed absurd. His magnificent tolerance to the woman shopper appeared farcical now, condescending and grandiose. He was holed up in heavy litter. That was the full extent of Ralph's splendour, and he knew it. And, obviously, so did Chail.

EIGHTEEN

'You can be Mr High-and-Mighty, Mr X.'

'Sir?' Harpur was used to getting unintelligible messages from the assistant chief's partially dangerous, questing mind, but could not recall anything of this tinge before. 'Sir?'

'Be outspoken and penetrative. Think of it as an extravaganza. A *jeu d'esprit*. As outspoken as you like.' A gorgeous thrum of totally unreliable friendship moved into Iles's tone. 'I trust you utterly.'

'Thank you, sir.'

'And I'm sure you would say absolutely ditto about me,' Iles remarked. 'We'll con the bastards,' he added. 'Kindly read this, would you, Col?' He handed Harpur a letter. It showed that Iles had somehow scrambled his way onto the shortlist for a chief constable post in Northern Britain. Harpur read quickly. He gathered that the ACC wanted to prepare himself by rehearsing the kind of interview he'd face, with Harpur playing the interviewing officer – Mr High-and-Mighty. Harpur didn't feel altogether at ease with this prospect. To be Harpur when Iles was Iles could be difficult enough, but to be Iles when he was actually Harpur and vice versa piled on the stress a bit.

Harpur had heard the rumours about Iles's possible future, of course. For instance, Intelligent had mentioned them, and occasionally Iles himself had given a hint or two that he might be trying for a new post. Harpur didn't think the ACC had spoken of that lately, though. It might be a tender subject if he'd had failures. Harpur didn't believe his affair with Sarah Iles had much to do with the assistant chief's alleged wish for a move. That was over, though Harpur knew the thought of it could still drive Iles half insane.

They were in Harpur's suite at headquarters, facing each other, Iles seated behind the big metal desk, Harpur opposite in his brown leather easy chair. Iles had suggested these positions, an applicant for the job uncomfortable and nervy, the interviewer dominant and relaxed. Almost certainly there would, in reality, be more than one interviewer – most likely a panel – but that couldn't be reproduced here. Harpur had to do.

Iles had on one of his £2,000–3,000 navy three-piece suits from his tailor, Dorking-Plain. There'd been a couple of minutes when Iles wanted to wear his ACC uniform for the rehearsal, but Harpur had talked him out of that. It could have led to confusion, and, in any case, Harpur knew that Iles would regard the post of chief constable as in some ways akin to a high office in the Diplomatic Corps or the Civil Service. He should dress accordingly. Uniforms put a bit of a gloss, and Iles liked a bit of a gloss, but he was aware that he liked a bit of a gloss and didn't often let it loose.

'Do you think this is the best way of dealing with the situation, sir, a mock-up interview?'

'Dealing with what situation, Col?'

'With preparing you for the job.'

'It's not a matter of preparing me for the job. It couldn't be more evident that I can handle the job,' Iles said.

'Oh.'

'It's to prepare me for dealing with *selection* for the job.'

'But these are related, aren't they, sir?'

'Which are?'

'Preparing for doing the job and preparing to deal with the selection to do the job.'

'Would they were,' Iles said.

'Would they were what?' Harpur said.

'Related.'

Harpur said: 'The selection system is surely devised to discover the man or woman most likely to make a success of the chiefship.'

'And you genuinely believe that, do you, Col?'

'Why else would the selection procedure exist, sir?'

'And yet I remain an assissssstant chief.' Iles still liked to speak his present job title under an excess of 's' sounds, to suggest it had no real substance, only slithering subordination.

The ACC became silent, as if he believed that these moments of theatre could be accomplished with all its detail as long as there was no crude, hostile interruption. Then he said: 'We must give Mr High-and-Mighty, Mr X a chance to speak.'

'How do you think your present workforce regard you?' Harpur as the interviewer said.

'Fondly, but with respect,' Iles said.

'Why fondly?'

'I'm that kind of person,' Iles said. 'I attract good feelings from others. I'm a magnet. They can't help it. And I, in turn, can't help affecting them like that. There's a reciprocity of admiration and affection.'

'Rumour tells me that quite a few of your people think you're a bit of a shit.'

Harpur, as Iles, thought for a moment that Iles as Iles was about to hit him. But then he said: 'I pity them.'

'Pity?' Harpur as Iles said.

'They are trapped inside cliché. They look at me and see only a boss. It's a thoughtless, robotic response.'

'I gather you have an exceptionally tranquil and well-conducted territory,' Harpur as Iles said. 'I suppose you claim this is largely due to you – ACC (Ops). Have you managed any distinguished Ops recently?'

'Leadership, I take it with me wherever I go. Just another flair. I get some occasional, temporary help from the head of CID, name of Harpur. Possibly you've heard of him. Perhaps he'll get an MBE, something worthy of that sort.'

'Yes, I've heard of him. He's rather brilliant, isn't he, in a quiet, modest, unpushing sort of way?'

NINETEEN

That malevolent business in the arcade – the filthy way Chail and his mate had pretended not to know him, or not to see him – this gave Ralph big worry. Perhaps they believed they'd fooled him. And perhaps, in a way, they had. It had been Ralph's aim to observe Chail unseen because Chail looked undoubtedly the most serious threat. The opposite had happened. All kinds of Ralph's plans and schemes would be trampled on and crushed. Additionally, but importantly, it infuriated Ralph that Chail should think it credible for anyone living in this area or nearby not instantly to see and recognize Ralph W. Ember, regardless of whether Ralph was possibly part-hidden by parked rubbish trucks. Chail was treating him, Ralph W. Ember, as if negligible.

Ralph never doubted, or hardly ever, that they had seen him, or that Chail had seen him and told his new companion that the one in the lorries-niche was their man. They both gave whatever was ahead a similar stiff-necked eyeballing. It was purposeful, and the purpose was to make out they hadn't seen Ralph and wouldn't have been interested in him if they had.

Where would those two go now? Were they already too distant for Ralph to hook onto them? And that wasn't the only question, was it? Where would he, Ralph, go now? That sounded straightforward enough. He knew the layout of the town very well. But it wasn't simple, was it? How could it be? He had been having a long-term peep at Chail when Chail had been having a long-term peep at him. It meant they'd been functioning in a circle. Ralph wondered whether if he quit the lorry hideaway and hurriedly tried to get behind that pair, he would eventually – or quicker than eventually – get behind himself, with Chail behind him.

He'd heard, hadn't he, that a while ago something like this had happened to cop, Harpur? Rumour at the time said

Harpur was thinking of retirement and considering a new career as private investigator. Apparently he'd been trying to remind himself of basic detection skills, such as tailing. But the whispers had said he'd finished by tailing himself.

It enraged Ralph to discover that he could fall into the same crazy error as a police officer. Ralph would admit that Harpur seemed to have some good bits to him, but mostly because he wasn't Iles. Ralph was Ralph W. Ember of Low Pastures, not someone brought down low to street level and fretting uselessly between dirt lorries. He found there was something especially idiotic about the Harpur tailing farce. And now Ralph would admit that this kind of pathetic disaster was not unique: Ralph W. Ember of Low Pastures could equal it, even beat it for awfulness.

'What the fuck you fucking well doing there?' One of the lorry drivers had come out of the shop and was blocking Ember's way to the pavement. He wasn't young. He wasn't too fit-looking. Ralph could have pushed him aside. That wasn't his mood now. He felt defeated. He found it hard to get words out.

'Who the fuck are you?' the lorry driver said.

That really hurt Ralph. This was someone ordinary and everyday who failed to recognize him. He wasn't putting on an act like Chail, behaving as though he didn't know who Ralph was. This was an entirely authentic, homespun nuisance voice, fucking nuisance voice, the kind of voice and terminology he didn't normally have to put up with these days. It had taken him a couple of decades and more to make it to such a nice spot and he wouldn't let it slip.

'Renovations?' Ralph replied, getting as much non-controversial sweetness into his voice as he could. 'So positive, so in tune with the future. Inspired – I don't think that's to overstate it. Did you notice those two?'

'Two what?'

'Like they were looking for someone, yet not looking for someone who was right in front of them.'

'What would that have to do with you and a lorry? You're in a nice tweedy three-piece suit,' the driver replied.

'Well, thank you, I'm sure,' Ralph said.

'So what you doing, so what you fucking doing nesting among debris?'

Ralph heard footsteps.

'Wow, it's Mr Ember, isn't it?' The other lorry driver and his mate had come out of the shop.

'Mr Ember?' the first driver said, sounding horrified at how he'd acted up till now.

'It is Mr Ralph Ember of Low Pastures, isn't it?' the second driver said.

'I didn't look properly, wasn't expecting anything like that.'

'You need to get some elocution lessons,' Ralph told him. He felt a good deal better now.

TWENTY

'I've been getting around some of my private local contacts,' Iles said.

'These are lucky people to get such consideration, sir,' Harpur said.

'I felt this was something that had to be done face to face,' Iles said.

'Thoughtful,' Harpur said.

'They'll have heard I won the chiefship elsewhere and will be moving on after the usual period of notice. I wanted to make the farewells personal and individual, not some generalized blurb.'

'Typically humane of you, sir.'

'One of these sources had something I would normally have kept confidential for at least a while. It's not a possibility I want to get involved with in this interim period, though. So I thought – am thinking – of you.'

'Good of you, sir.'

'Oh, I don't know. I owe you hugely.'

'Yes?' Harpur said.

'You did your best to hurl the worst possible crap at me in our interview rehearsal, so anything that came in the real one seemed praise. I could keep cool and indomitable. A winner. So you see, Col, you're not the only one to have very useful secret tipsters, informants,' Iles said.

'No, perhaps not, sir,' Harpur said.

'How do you mean?' Iles said.

'How do I mean what, sir?'

'You said "perhaps not". How do you mean "perhaps not"?' Iles said.

'Oh, it's just something that might come up in conversation,' Harpur replied.

'What might?' Iles said.

'"Perhaps not",' Harpur said, 'Not much more than a tick.'

'Which conversation?' Iles said.

'This one, sir,' Harpur said.

'You mean that perhaps not everyone has a secret whisperer?' Iles said.

'There's a lot of it about,' Harpur said.

'What?'

'Whispering.'

'You know the Courtway Arcade? Lovely commercial thoroughfare?'

'Oh, yes,' Harpur said.

'I have a source in the arcade. Greengrocer.'

'Ideal. Everything looks innocent there – lettuce, beans, chestnuts.'

'He sees quite a load of interesting life.'

'I expect so,' Harpur said.

'Occasionally it's to the point,' Iles said. 'I thought some of it might be your sort of stuff, Col. Not dangerous, or even potentially dangerous, inherently routine and go-nowhere. Exactly right for you. The human digestion demands greens. There's a criss-cross of many people there.'

'Protein,' Harpur said.

'Ralph,' Iles replied.

'In the arcade?'

'There's something going on, Col.' They were talking in Harpur's room again.

'Something going on in the arcade?' Harpur said.

'In the arcade and something bigger than that – much bigger.'

'To do with the greengrocery?'

'I believe it's something a twerp like you wouldn't be able to handle once I've taken over in the new job.'

'I'll try,' Harpur said.

'Of course you will. That's how you are, Col. Someone who'll always have a go, admirable in its way, its terribly limited way. You might ask, I suppose, why you, a chief super, are not invited to step into my job when I go.'

'No, I wouldn't ask that.'

'Why not, Col?'

'I wouldn't. They'll bring in someone to replace you here. He/she might have that holy knack. Instinct.'

'A mouth, good at going on TV to explain away some catastrophic failure. She/he will stifle any frail talent you might have brought to things, Col.'

'And all this involves Ralph Ember, does it?' Harpur said.

'My source recognizes him. Everyone in this city would, I guess. My source actually hears him speak to someone.'

'Plenty of chit-chat there. Something worthwhile was bound to show. That's why we have such a network, isn't it, sir?'

'Which network?'

'Whisperers. Informants.'

Iles was in the easy chair this time, and Harpur behind his desk. Iles had on a tan outfit, perhaps because he was going later to one of the farming unions about rustling.

He had a way of arranging himself among the cushioned back and fat, stuffed arms that must suggest a kind of denial of this luxury while actually having it. Iles was slight, bordering on skimpy. He sat huddled in the left back corner of the chair. He looked as if he feared the building could collapse soon, and he might escape the worst of it by folding himself away on the edge. He appeared to radiate deference and acute vulnerability, which Harpur knew to be wholesale bollocks.

Iles was chief constable elect to that Force up north, but he didn't crow. Some would be surprised at that. Not Harpur. He reckoned Iles wanted a few more chances to pronounce his present rank with all the rotten glut of 's' sounds – assssissssstant chief. It would be wasteful not to get the maximum out of this crude attempt at oratory.

Harpur thought how splendid and terrible to lose him. Harpur had heard before anyone else that he had clinched the distant top post. Iles had texted Harpur: 'The cunts have caved in and we've done it, Col.' Apparently they'd asked him word for word one of the questions Harpur had used in the mock-up: 'Mr Iles, rumour has it that some people in your team think you're a career shit.'

Iles had apparently amended the answer he'd come up with at the rehearsal: 'Only some?' he'd said in this new, crucial reality reply. 'I should do better than that, and will be trying to accomplish something different in the new appointment when I get it.' Members of the panel had chuckled warmly at this snarling boldness, Iles told Harpur.

Now, in Harpur's room at headquarters, the assistant chief reached into the breast pocket of his jacket and brought out a few sheets of paper clipped together. 'I'd like you to have a look at these, Harpur.'

'Certainly sir.'

'But bear in mind he is not the artist, he is a source and greengrocer. They are the picture as he saw it, but not a whole picture, part of a picture from which you, or someone like you, if that is not unthinkable, can begin a deep, deeper search. But you'll be familiar with this kind of development: information arrives in segments and may, or may not, be fitted to other segments to give a wholeness. If we were composing an academic paper on the history and nature of informing – and why not? – this would be our starting point, our theme.'

Iles stood, without any help from the chair arms, and crossed the room to put the papers on the desk in front of Harpur. He did this carefully, almost religiously and continued to stand at the desk gazing down on the pieces of paper while Harpur smoothed them out alongside each other, a kind of ritual.

The papers appeared to be lined pages torn from an A4 exercise book. Harpur hated to see what he thought of as school writing books ripped apart. It seemed to him the beginnings of chaos, a terrible barbarism. But, of course, exercise books were probably on their way out in schools. Children worked on screens now. This was the twenty-first century.

Iles bent forward and, with his right hand, gave Harpur some help. Harpur copied the solemnity. Their hands briefly – very briefly – touched on the central paper, Harpur's left, Iles's right. Harpur thought it must be the closest he and the ACC had ever been. He was glad it happened, not on account of the paper lying more neatly and tidily, but because the contact would stick in Harpur's mind as a very vivid reminder of Iles, career shit or not. Like those imagined panellists, Harpur would have a chuckle at the cheek to be recalled in so much of Iles's life.

Iles withdrew his hand, as though a deposit had been paid

for it and the time just ran out. He straightened up, turned and went back to his chair and sat down. Harpur moved along the three sheets of paper and then back again, like someone making a choice of cheeses at a supermarket display. He was aware of being watched hard, continuously. Iles had a warmish smile on, as warm a smile as it ever was going to be with Iles. Harpur felt that the ACC and he were in a kind of smart alliance. He didn't greatly like this: too entwined.

'What see you there, Col?' Iles said.

A number of straight lines had been drawn in pencil to form three long coffin-like open-topped boxes. One of these on each piece of paper, then two of them lying together, almost touching, on the third. In the small gap between the two of these on this third sheet was what seemed to Harpur a sketched matchstick man – a human figure miniaturized and done in straight lines. Its toy-room arms were bent up in front of itself – an attempt to hide its face?

'Fascinating,' Harpur said.

'I thought it would take hold of a mind like yours, Harpur.'

'Which is that, sir?'

'Capable? No question. Tough? No question. Driven? No question. Gifted? That's another matter though. We've had these discussions many a time, yes?'

'I wouldn't say they were discussions,' Harpur replied. 'Diktats. You told me what I was.'

Iles ignored this. 'Do you see Ralph there?'

'Where?'

'The papers. As we said at the beginning, this cannot be a complete picture. My source doesn't know why Ralph is in the arcade, so neither do we. He says that at one point Ralph seemed to be aghast at something or somebody. But my source cannot explain it. He has done this quick drawing of the scene there, hoping a meaning will surface.'

'There's only one human form present: a matchstick man.'

'Good, good, Col. You're right, there is only one human form. Therefore, if we are searching for signs of people here, this one must be it.'

'We don't know either why its arms are bent upwards like that.'

'Excellent,' Iles said. 'We don't. I knew you'd get there. That figure has Ralph Ember written all over it.'

'Does it?'

'Oh, you're still puzzled, are you, Col? I told my source always to keep a watch for Ralph Ember after that episode at Low Pastures in the night.'

'Are you working from what we spoke of earlier – instinct, sir?'

'I don't need instinct. I have a source. Think lorries, Col.'

'Lorries?'

'Dumpers.'

'You mean that Ralph – the mini-Ralph, that is – is standing between parked lorries – mini-lorries – for the sketch.'

'Great, Col.'

'Parked lorries in the arcade for some work?' Harpur said. 'That's what these straight-line, box-type items in the sketch are, is it?'

'Terrific, Col.'

'Why was Ralph in the arcade at all?'

'I've told you the source didn't give me that. There was a woman shopper with some items she'd bought, so the source could tell me as much, but it's of no significance. Ralph speaks to her and she replies. My source thinks "Sodding" or "Sod" in the reply but can't give me more. There was a bit of trouble with one of the drivers.'

Harpur said: 'He'd be pissed off, I imagine, finding someone hanging about his vehicle to no apparent decent purpose. Our boy might think he'd better protect his face, in case of a coming thump. So, the arm up.'

'Your mastery of this situation is breathtakingly perceptive, Col. You've blown the illustration wide open single-handed.'

'Well, I'd say I had quite a bit of help,' Harpur said.

'Yes, you would say it, not stay cleverly, egocentrically and deceitfully quiet about how your successes were in fact achieved, which is why you'll never make it to assistant chief.'

Next day Harpur went alone to the arcade. He was restless, a state that could afflict him occasionally. He worried about two main developments that wouldn't slacken their hold. They were developments which, in a strange sense, cancelled each other out. They still had enough in them, though, to give him deep unease.

At home he thought he had hidden this edginess pretty well from Denise and the children, but then Jill, leaving for school in the morning, had said: 'What's up, Dad?'

'Ah, that's almost a film title, isn't it?' Play the dumbo, Harpur thought. It might make Jill feel sorry for him and try some extra tenderness. No.

'Of course it's a film,' Jill said. '*What's Up, Doc?* Re-runs of it get on to the ancient movies channel – your vintage. But why are you dodging the question?'

'Am I?'

'You know you are.'

'Do I?' Harpur said.

'Acute jumpiness about something,' Jill said.

'Jumpiness?'

'Tenseness.'

'Really?'

'OK, OK, Dad. You're not going to talk. I can't win.'

'Talk about what?'

'That I'd like to discover, but I'm reaching nowhere, aren't I? I've been going over in my head for possibles. Nothing. Have to go. Can't hang about, to get brick-walled. Is it anxiety in case you're forced to deal with something you can't manage?' Jill said. 'But, yes you can.' She kissed him on the side of his head and whispered: 'You'll cope OK. As ever, Dad. We believe in you. Is it to do with the wharf body?'

'Is what to do with it?'

'Oh, don't start again, Dad.'

Watching her bustle off to her classes, Harpur took pleasure in the regularity of this term-time ritual. Hazel was also part of it but had gone on ahead. Harpur thought Iles could be very wrong when he doubted Harpur's ability to safeguard the city's nice orderliness. It would be tough without Iles, though not doomed.

Harpur and Jill were in the porch at Arthur Street, Jill with a haversack of school books, lunch sandwiches and a can of ginger beer. He'd go later to the Courtway. Harpur didn't get rapture from arcades, as Iles did. They seemed to Harpur like tunnels with a glass roof. The sound of people's shoes was magnified in them and, given a sort of rapid slap tone, seemed to suggest a desperate urgency as they shopped, or tried to get beautified in one of the three very well-meant salons.

Although Harpur didn't experience a glow from arcades, he did agree with Iles that they were very suitable for tipsters, and he had a source in the Courtway himself, though not one he mentioned to Iles. He was the arcade janitor and had a little den with his gear near the south entrance.

Perhaps this time Harpur would see something he'd missed previously, and, more significantly, that Iles had missed. Maybe Harpur could put a degree of light on the 'something' that Iles sensed was going on. Harpur would get high-quality joy from solving this teaser – joy and bitchiness at having done what Iles couldn't.

First of those two factors able to upset Harpur was Iles's blunt declaration that something was going on.

Second, there came Iles's admission – twice – that he didn't know what it was. Harpur found himself utterly unused to this kind of sequence. If Iles diagnosed in his mysterious style that something was going on, something would in fact be going on and, given a while – generally a very little while – Iles would find out what and deal with it, usually something bad or very bad or toweringly bad or inadequate. Now, though, there was no such resolution and Harpur felt at a loss and feeble. Perhaps Iles was correct to doubt his ability. He couldn't have let Jill know about his large-scale worry, though she and possibly Hazel had spotted the symptoms. He'd found he needed another look at the arcade, and a look carried out solo.

It dazed Harpur slightly to realize that not only was Iles due to move away soon, but even before that his powers here seemed to be shrinking. Harpur knew he was absent today, possibly getting a familiarizing tour of what would be his new ground as chief. Harpur didn't want him to know of this second visit. It would question Iles's magic. The ACC – almost chief – was not someone to be checked up on by a minion.

'It could be nothing at all, Mr Harpur,' his source said.

'That's always how information comes to us, Lance.' Harpur

did what could have been an Iles echo: 'We deal in segments. On their own they could be nothing at all. Fitted together they occasionally make something. Not always. Occasionally.' Harpur knew he must sound like lecture notes or that academic paper Iles had spoken of. Perhaps most police who ran informants were keen to give the practice a respectable, even elevated flavour, because they knew that in reality it was quite a shady, shameful game. Harpur himself felt a little like that sometimes.

'Sketchy – so sketchy – I didn't feel it right to bother you, not in the present state of things,' Lance said.

'What do you mean, Lance, "in the present state of things"?'

'Power fights,' Lance said.

'Are there power fights?' Harpur said.

'Coming. On their way,' Lance replied.

'Segments,' Harpur said. 'They don't make anything much until they're fitted together, if ever. We have to accept the "if ever" caution. But as the segments fall into place next to other segments, we get a lovely sense of all of them destined to make up the desired fullness. They have that potential waiting in them, ready to be herded together to make a greatly wanted unit.'

Harpur knew that if Hazel and/or Jill heard him spout this kind of preposterous blah they'd turn queasy yellow from nausea, but Lance was much easier to satisfy with these woozy, cheerful, bullshit notions. He was over seventy, not in great health, glad to be in a dolly job with a tipster sideline, and not inclined to initiate upset. 'I do see some activity, oh yes,' Lance said.

'Where?'

'Here – the arcade.'

'What activity?' Harpur said.

'You.'

'Me?'

'You're part of the activity.'

'What's the other part, Lance?'

'You'd be the most important of them, if I might say.'

'More important than who?' Harpur said.

'Whom?' Lance said. 'My grandchildren correct me if I say who when it should be whom.'

'My daughters are like that,' Harpur said.

'It's old-fashioned and pompous to get it right,' Lance said.

'Whom, then, do you mean is part of the activity, beside myself?'

'Ralph Ember. You've heard of him, I expect. Ralph W. Ember of Low Pastures. Among those lorries over there to do with rebuilding. A lot of dust for someone like me to clean up, except it's not just like me, it's me. Activity. Which I could do without.'

They were in Lance's lair, surrounded by heavy-duty brooms, watering cans, buff-coloured hoses, fire extinguishers. Lance opened a couple of folding canvas chairs for them.

'And was there further activity, Lance, not just me and Ralph Ember and the rebuilding murk?'

'What was Ralph staring at?' Lance replied. 'This is where matters get complicated and very obscure.'

'Was he staring?'

'At two blokes walking through the arcade, walking very . . . well, very thrustful. One of them I've seen around. Name of Chail, is it?'

'There is a lad called Chail known to us,' Harpur said.

'He's with a beardy, not someone I know. I don't think he's been here before. He's the sort I'd remember.'

'And they are both staring at Ralph?' Harpur said.

'No.'

'Only one staring?' Harpur asked.

'Neither.'

'He's staring at them, but they don't respond?' Harpur said.

'Right. That's why I said it wasn't worth calling you about. Nothing happened.'

'Nothing happening is something happening. The nothing-ness of it becomes something,' Harpur said.

'Ah,' Lance said.

'What?' Harpur replied.

'That's why I'm here,' Lance said. 'You can look at nothing and turn it into something. I can see what you mean. The fact that nothing happens tells you something. But I couldn't have thought of that.'

'I'm here as well,' Harpur said.

'Not the way I'm here.'

'Which way is that?' Harpur replied.

Lance leaned forward in his chair to touch a couple of yard brushes and a wheelbarrow. 'Me. I'm with this stuff every day. It's my job. You just drop by once in a while with a smart analysis. It doesn't last very long.'

'What you see is very valuable to me,' Harpur said.

'You can interpret. That's your job. You work out what things mean. These tools are just tools for sprucing up the arcade. It can't be done without them. Their limit, though. The arcade is useful to you. It runs through the main part of the city and gives you a show.'

'What d' you think these activities mean, Lance?'

'When I mentioned the staring and the negative staring, I see you perk up. Your face gets all interested and alert. I've strayed on to your area though I hardly knew it. What I have to think, Mr Harpur, is I saw this staring game, observing it for as long as it lasted, but I didn't think it worth giving you a ring about it, although I'm a source. There's something missing in me, and what it is is the ability to see what something signifies, or might signify. It's no wonder I'm among the cleaning items. I can't do probing and speculating. To me a watering can is a watering can.'

'You're the one who started me wondering,' Harpur said. 'I'd be nowhere otherwise, and I'd still be nowhere.'

'What do you think it means, Mr Harpur?'

'What?'

'Ralph. The stare.'

'I don't know.'

'That's your task, isn't it?'

'What?' Harpur said.

'To interpret.'

'You can do some deducing too, Lance.'

'Ralph's scared,' Lance said. 'That's what I pick up.'

'Possibly,' Harpur said.

'He was standing between a couple of lorries, wasn't he?' Harpur said.

'Ah,' Lance said.

'What?' Harpur said.

'You know this already?'

'Some of it,' Harpur said.

'How?'

'That's what I meant when I said information comes in segments. We're talking about one of the segments.'

'So what is Ralph scared of?' Lance asked.

'I don't know,' Harpur said.

'His business?' Lance said. 'Anxious re the business? He's had trouble like that before, hasn't he?' Lance sighed. 'But this is me doing a think, isn't it? I'm a janitor.'

'A janitor who thinks,' Harpur said. 'Ralph runs into envy. Naturally he does.'

Lance nodded a couple of times. 'He's asking for it – again without knowing what the possible trouble is.' He paused. He put a hand on the wheelbarrow again, maybe to remind himself of his job. 'Mr Harpur, I think if I was someone from outside, looking at it like someone new would see it, I would think, what a lovely spot this is; not only the arcade, although, yes, the arcade is lovely, but I mean in general. And that would be right. I admit a smashed skull at the sand and gravel wharf is something else, but mostly, averagely, it's a sweet city, rich in tranquillity and all the protected goodnesses.'

'Yes, it's OK,' Harpur replied.

'Oh, OK is not enough, surely Mr Harpur, if I might respectfully demur.'

'OK-plus then,' Harpur replied.

'Begrudging a bit, still.'

'What are you saying, Lance?'

'Do I sound a trifle fascist, Mr Harpur? The corporate state – people defined by their jobs and compelled to stay in them?'

'That's a depressing idea.'

'So we have this Chail, who does a bit on the substances side as a dealer if I hear right?'

'Yes, you probably hear right.'

'He knows what things are like here, very comfortable and more or less safeish; but his companion – he's the new pair of eyes that I mentioned. He needs to be given a tour and a sight of it with commentary from someone quite clued-up from his own business firm, but who's thinking a possible major increase. Is Mr Chail mooting a partnership with Mr Beardie? This arcade visit is important. What is it they say, Mr Harpur?'

'Who – not whom?'

'The experts.'

'Which?'

'Fiscal gurus. What they say is "Expand or go under". No alternative. No standing still.'

Lance paused again, stayed silent for a minute, and then started to speak once more: 'But you'll . . .' He shrugged, seemed about to go into another silence. He resumed, though: 'But you'll be saying to yourself, Mr Harpur, this geezer spends his time mostly locked up with the garden-type clobber, so when someone comes along, such as you, Mr Harpur, who does know a watering can when he sees one but is also able to do conversation, then this nothing-much handyman finds there's something to be said for this talking lark. Yes, something to be said is said, so off he goes, unstoppable, jabber, jabber, jabber, quaint words like "mooting" and "thrustful", "demur", spiel upon spiel. I'm sorry, Mr Harpur. Blame the dustpans.'

'No, that's not how it is, Lance. It's all very helpful and clear.'

Harpur, considering retirement and the need for a replacement career, wondered if he could learn how to be a fiscal guru.

'Chail didn't want any interference from Ralph at that moment and so the staring ahead, plus, of course, to put Ralph devastatingly off-balance because apparently ignored.'

'I don't know what that's about. I don't understand it,' Harpur said.

'I see a sort of spreading shambles, not one I can put right with a squirt or two from the hose.'

'We depend on you and people like you. We'll win.'

'Mr Iles is going, I'm told.'

'That will make me even more dependent on you, Lance.'

'I can't compensate for the loss of Mr Iles,' Lance said. 'His sort don't come in a catalogue.'

'But we'll have a go at it, won't we?'

'Of course, you've got other sources, haven't you – big-timers, Mr Harpur?'

'Stay well, Lance.'

TWENTY-ONE

R
alph Ember found there were moments when he thought
of his property and estate almost as if they were human,
and not just human but human enemies. He would never
have believed this possible. But yet it had happened. It had
unquestionably happened. The feeling took in the whole
building and acreage, including the recent extension.

As a matter of fact, he was outside the extension now, and
the sense of unfriendliness was at its strongest. His displeasure
was not to do with the taste/style of the renovations. These
were high-falutin' considerations – snob considerations, which
he'd admit might have commandeered his attention previously,
but which seemed of next-to-no importance today. What he
had to think was how easy it would be to kill him or a member
of his family, if he or she were standing where he stood now.
After that idiotic incident on ladders up at the roof, plenty of
people knew about the layout at Low Pastures, not all of these
people well-disposed. There was a door directly into the gallery
to serve the extension, and separate from the main entrance
hall to Low Pastures, and Ralph had always worried about it.
He thought it too remote. Anyone using that door to go for
a walk around the estate would be wonderfully framed as a
target.

The architect looking after the extension work had persuaded
Ralph to let him include the door, though. His argument was
that the extension served as a kind of gallery for Ralph's china
collection, and he might want to take visitors into that section
to see the splendid items and sets without having to squire
them around the rest of the house. The word 'squire' had
greatly attracted Ralph. He liked the idea of having this type
of status and able to confer the favour of a privileged look at
the china collection, but not allow any further hobnobbing.

The point was, wasn't it, that the strange encounter
with Chail and his mate in the arcade had forcefully and

bewilderingly changed all the major expectations of Ralph's life. Up until that frightening incident in the arcade, Ralph had thought of himself as very much in charge of how things were for him, and how they would be in the future. He was Ralph Ember of Low Pastures. He was the one who kept a watch, undetected, on someone who had come to seem a likely menace. Ralph did the watching, was certainly not the passive object, the targeted item. That's how he saw things.

But now he had to realize the facts were the opposite, and he'd better cater for this drastically changed situation. Because Chail and his friend had behaved as if they didn't recognize him, or even see him, it made matters worse, showing that they did see and recognize him and had a very dangerous motive for acting as if they didn't: that is, dangerous for Ralph. This was why he'd come to regard Low Pastures as a liability, not at all as previously a glorious asset. That pair hadn't wanted to alert him, so they gave what the old politician used to call 'the big ignoral'.

He was standing with his back to the house and stepped a dozen paces forward into the grounds before turning, so that he could get a full sight of the frontage of the Low Pastures property. He knew this from previous use of the spot, but added a few more yards so that the scene would take in the extension. With this adjustment, the view was perfectly complete, and it restored some of his fondness for the spread. It was absurd, surely, to blame the estate of Low Pastures because things had turned rough for Ralph. The loveliness and dignity of the house and extension were there for him. Ralph reckoned that not many would appreciate the elegant splendour of Low Pastures as much as he usually did, and as he did again now. But he felt this wonderful construction could be taken from him, if someone hunted him and wiped out his business, wiped out himself, perhaps. Of course he'd had this feeling before. Low Pastures had a fine history, but there was also a recent period when it was rented out by the then owners to a very notable villain, Caring Oliver.

That kind of impermanence was always in Ralph's mind. He lived in a borderland between commerce and criminality, as did many others, not all of these in the House of Lords.

After all, he could be regarded as a very notable villain himself. But he owned, not rented, Low Pastures, and owned it without a mortgage. This helped make Caring's period here only a blip, not part of Low Pastures' true character. Ralph, in fact, relied on this true character of the property to lift him out of crook category, though he was not stupid and recognized that without the marvellous illegal wealth from his commodities business, he would not have been able to buy and extend Low Pastures, with or without a mortgage, nor his social club, The Monty.

He'd often experienced worrying uncertainty about his home and business but never as acutely as now. He was conscious of his sight of the house blurring somehow and suddenly knew he was weeping. That made him proud. More confusion. It showed a heartfelt and noble regard for the Low Pastures possessions. People looking at the house and its territory must reason that only someone who had the taste and wealth and stalwart character to chime with the obvious fine qualities on show here could be the proprietor of this gem: a radiant suitability, surely.

Ralph did acknowledge to himself, occasionally, or more often than occasionally, that there might be a huge fault in this rickety attempt at logic. After all, Hitler probably had a nice, dinky place up in the mountains, but that couldn't make him any sweeter. It was a brilliantly comforting idea, though, and deserved an airing, if only briefly. Ralph would provide it as often as he could for himself. He had to meet the standard imposed by his estate. Gazing at Low Pastures now, he decided he could be said to feel at home with large-scale ideas and concepts.

It was a habit of his to come home between morning and late-night stints at The Monty. Margaret must have seen him from a window, dawdling in the grounds, and came out to join Ralph. She used the main entrance to the house. It was mid-afternoon on a sunny May day. He imagined what it might be like if someone were gunning for Margaret as a means of hurting him. Bushes and hedges gave intermittent cover on her approach, but there possibly wasn't enough of it. He wiped the tears away from his cheeks with the backs of his hands.

'Ralph! Have you been blubbing, you poor creature?'

'Blubbing?' he replied. 'No, no.' He had a good laugh as if amazed at the notion. 'The sun hurts my eyes.'

'All quiet and gracious on The Monty front?' she said. He found he was still trying to work out in his mind the kind of sniping angles that might be used against Margaret one day. He had to take care of her and the children. That resolve never left him and never dwindled. It would be doubly terrible if any of his family were gunned down in the revered surroundings of Low Pastures, or even inside the house itself – the TV room, modernized kitchen, or his business office. This contained all his files and profit-and-loss accounts as a transaction facilitator – supposing there ever were losses.

But he had hardly any qualms about allowing her free rein of such a sensitive area. This, after all, was the twenty-first century. A wife definitely deserved some privileges, especially the kind of talented wife Margaret had turned out to be. 'Transaction facilitator' was a mouthful. It meant he fixed deals. This was no minor skill. Some of these negotiations became very heated.

They had another downstairs room they called the library, though it had on the shelves only what Ralph regarded as quite ordinary paperbacks, some car manuals and a couple of textbooks for that foundation year as a mature student on his university course; in suspension now because of business pressures. These seemed to be increasing all the time, though still without precise shape. But an increase was an increase.

'If you've been crying, Ralph,' Margaret said, 'it would be something I'd understand totally.'

'Crying?' Ralph replied. 'Am I a baby?' It niggled him to be sympathized with by her.

'It was as if it had surprised you, this reaction, this weeping – overwhelmed you. I hate to see you like that. Ralph Ember of Low Pastures is not such a person.'

'True,' Ralph said.

'But . . .'

'Is there a but?'

'I think there is,' Margaret said.

'Oh!'

'Because I believe you *were* crying. And the thing is . . . the real thing is, I know why. OK, it's still Ralph W. Ember of Low Pastures, and the location is, in fact, Low Pastures, but this doesn't mean that Ralph W. Ember can't have certain feelings, does it Ralph? And I see good cause for those feelings, irresistible cause for these feelings. I wonder if you know what I'm getting at, Ralph?' He knew what she was getting at. It was what he would like to get at himself. It was what had brought on that unstoppable rush of tears.

She waved her arm to take in everything – the house, the extension, the grounds, the cars parked near the main front door. The pool, tennis courts and stables were behind the house but Ralph reckoned she meant them as well. 'It's all so lovely,' she said. 'You cry out of joy and wonderment.'

'Yes.' But he feared it might all be snatched from him: others envied that loveliness, acquisitively envied it. He believed they regarded it as an insult that he kept it from them – flaunted it, in their opinion.

'So completely beautiful,' she said.

'Yes.'

'And you, Ralph, so completely right for it all and vice versa.'

'Some comparison, Margaret!'

'But spot on. Anyone would see it.'

It was the kind of thinking he had dismissed as inflated tommyrot only a little while ago. But Ralph said nothing to correct her. She had joyfully presented him with this thought, obviously believing it was new and special to her, and he considered it would be monstrously cruel to reject it. She did another wave with her right arm involving the same areas and items and then lowered it and took hold of Ralph's in a good, reassuring style. She nodded towards one of the thick, tall, evergreen hedges nearby, marking off the end of a croquet lawn.

He gazed all around and could see no gardeners. They must be working behind the house. The children were still at school. Ralph gave a gentle pull on the sleeve of Margaret's blouse and they moved towards the dense hedge, Ralph's arm around her now. It wasn't the first time they had made love close to these nicely fashioned roots, including even as late one year as Christmas week. It was a more apt climate today. Probably the gardeners were in the tulip beds at the back.

In any case, Margaret and Ralph didn't strip entirely. Ralph reckoned that nakedness wasn't essential for sincerity, and he could supply plenty of sincerity, regardless of how he was dressed or half-dressed. Dropped trousers could have their own integrity, and the gentle sound of his braces hitting the ground entranced him. Perhaps, after all, she was right, and the grandeur of the setting did call for and get equivalent magnificence from him, not that daft temporary dislike.

They tucked themselves in under the lowest branch of the hedge. It wasn't just for concealment. They could find here a fresh-air sweetness and feel the strong companionship of nature. Ralph felt that nature had enough acceptable qualities to deserve his companionship. Margaret said: 'If you were kicked out of the property, Ralph, I'd have a new name and identity for you.'

'Yes? What?'

'Al,' she said.

'Al what? Capone?'

'Al Fresco-Fucker.'

'Rarely, but worth the wait.'

'All this is yours, Ralph. It can't, in fact be taken away from you.'

'It's ours,' he replied.

'If you say so. Kind,' she said. 'And there's absolutely no call for tears.'

The gardeners would be too far off to hear anything of the pleasured wolf-brand howling and urgent, high-pitched boiled-kettle-type scream. Afterwards Margaret and Ralph brushed each other down.

'You make me determined and reliable, Maggie.' But an al-fresco fuck couldn't really solve everything. Ralph's fears remained, even if the tears didn't.

'You underestimate yourself, Ralph. In some ways the modesty is admirable.'

'It used to bore me paralytic when people kept saying I resembled the young Charlton Heston,' he replied.

'Which you do. But I and others want to go deeper. We respect something solid and courageous.'

'Thank you, Maggie.'

They made their way back towards the main porch and doors of the house. They walked slowly. They were close but Ralph didn't have an arm around her now. Ralph thought that kind of thing could be overdone. Good marriages didn't need it. If you'd brushed first-grade soil off someone's clothes, this of itself was a statement of devotion.

In any case, his feelings at present were different from hers. He stopped and turned around to look towards the gates and the road. He wanted to get a more settled, careful view of where exactly the shot, shots, might come from if Margaret was targeted one day when she made her way across the front lawns, shielded at some moments by the bushes and hedges, including the love hedge.

She paused alongside him, though she couldn't know why Ralph had pulled up. Maybe she believed he simply needed a confirmation of the grand elegance of the view from the house, a reminder always gloriously available for him and Margaret. He saw nothing unusual, in fact saw nothing that moved. It was like a beautiful picture. He did hear a car or van engine, though, a car that seemed to be approaching Low Pastures and slowing. It was out of sight for the moment behind trees that bordered the estate.

Ralph tensed. Part of him realized this might be absurd: all kinds of vehicles – entirely unthreatening vehicles – came to Low Pastures. Margaret had a lot of stuff delivered. OK, OK, a car was approaching and reducing speed. So what? Did it seem a special, unfavourable kind of slowing? Did it bring big and dangerous possibilities? Ralph wondered, and yes, also tensed up. There'd been a time when this kind of special alertness was more or less routine for him. Some enemies had been obstructive and needed deterring, or if the circumstances were unresolvable, shot. This was very much a family home now and the circumstances were different. He had a family's ordinary needs.

He saw nothing unusual when he did his eyeballing. In fact, he still saw nothing that moved. Ralph rarely carried a gun these days, and hardly ever around Low Pastures. A current distaste for firearms and bullets governed his life lately and made him decide to deal with any menace by hand, skin-on-skin, as it were. But now he did feel this had come to seem hopelessly precious and tangled when seen against practicalities. He found he longed for a pistol as he and Margaret stared towards the Low Pastures open gates. She had obviously heard the car too, and glanced at Ralph to see his reactions. She appeared to share his anxiety, then looked back towards the road and gates.

Ralph had consciously to stop himself patting his jacket pockets, as if about to locate and produce a gun. He knew depressingly well that there was no gun. Margaret would know it too. She could often read him accurately, despite his efforts to disguise something stupid and embarrassing. She would realize that Ralph was off-balance and disturbed, was idiotically searching for help where no help could possibly be found now, only on offer years ago at a period when Ralph was somebody different, with other trappings and accessories.

In the past he would have used a shoulder holster. Only the sleekest of automatics could fit into a jacket pocket without causing a giveaway bulge. When Ralph went with a pistol aboard in those rougher times, he would have avoided that crudeness, so his action now was nonsensical twice over, searching for a non-existent gun, and standing shakily with Margaret, waiting to see what this car's business might be – maybe nothing much at all to worry about, perhaps the week's supermarket deliveries.

Ralph thought he would have recognized the engine sound of any really distinguished car, say a Ferrari or even a Jaguar. A Bentley or Rolls would have next-to-no engine noise at all, of course. This vehicle made quite an amount of noise, though seemingly not doing very much in the way of progress.

A dark red Peugeot saloon, a few years old and not very spruce, travelling at about ten miles an hour, appeared in the gateway and came on into the grounds at the same speed. The driver gave two short toots on the horn as greeting. Ralph didn't recognize the bearded companion of Bernard Chail behind the wheel, with Chail himself in the passenger seat,

The car stopped and he lowered his window. He leaned out and gave a cheery prolonged wave to Margaret and Ralph. 'Wonderful to see you, Ember!' he called. 'And your lady, too, of course. Where are my manners?'

Neither Margaret nor Ralph waved back. 'Who are these people, Ralph?' she said.

'I'll deal with it,' he replied.

'Yes, but who are they?'

Chail said: 'I believe Mrs Ember is puzzled. Shall I tell you what I see?'

'No thanks,' Ralph said. 'Could you please go and see it somewhere else?'

'What I see is two admirable folk, possibly post-recent-intimacy, enjoying pleasured moments flanked by beautiful symbols of their success, namely the Low Pastures edifice.'

'Are you pissed?' Margaret replied. 'Whether or not, fuck off out of here.'

'We'd hoped to make contact earlier,' Chail said. 'Did Ralph tell you about the arcade? We'd have liked him to follow us out to somewhere confidential on that day.'

'Out of where?' Margaret said.

'The arcade, of course,' Chail said. 'But he's too wily. We realize we are dealing with someone considerable. Phone certainly won't do. I don't mean just the magnificence of the property, though the property is a factor, bound to be – the china collection, the children's ponies and the pool, together with the actual building.'

Chail bent his left arm out of the car window, made a fist and brought it down to give the door a couple of hard blows – exasperated, ashamed blows. 'But look here, you're listening intently to me, but I know that if you were to respond it would be with one unfriendly word, "bullshit!" The flattery does nothing to make my approach to you stronger and more convincing.'

'Absolutely not, so get lost,' Margaret said.

'I'm pretty certain you two can sense that there are crucial changes due in the business scene here,' Chail replied. 'Why I said we'd hoped to make contact earlier.'

He withdrew his arm. 'Instability,' he said. 'We have to

cater for instability, potential instability. The possibilities are infinite, and very daunting.'

That sort of word – 'instability' – satisfied Ralph. It was a proper commercial dealings word and he could take it three times if necessary. 'Potential' went with it OK. It had a fragment of subtlety to it – a bit of a go at forecasting.

Chail, smiling genially, got out of the car. As if following this prompt, the driver did too. They seemed to feel they would be asked into the house to carry on the conversation more comfortably.

But Margaret said: 'So goodbye, both.'

Ralph felt strangely impressed by the cockiness of these two, though. It almost matched the attitude Iles could take now and then. He found himself wondering whether perhaps, after all, they had something genuinely new, genuinely useful. He admired their attempt to lure him out from the arcade when he heard about it. That was subtlety.

'Reputation,' Chail said. 'Other firms all over Britain, maybe even in France and Holland, try hard to model their companies on yours and Manse Shale's. I mean the steadiness and civility. And I suppose, too, the kind of status that can bring possession of a splendid, generally admired estate like this one.' He gestured with one hand towards the house and the setting. There'd be sentries at night, wouldn't there?

Ralph thought Margaret might have spotted that his reaction to these two was altering, perhaps had already altered, had softened, had become more positive. He sensed that she might be reshaping her own estimate of them. That was how things often were with Margaret: she would swap or amend her views on something so they squared with his. It was one of her most loveable qualities. But it wasn't just a matter of love. She knew there were people in Ralph's work that she could not know properly, or truly know at all. These two were in that category. She had to take her lead from Ralph in her attitude.

Chail said: 'It's why Donald is with me, isn't it? He'd heard of developments here – well, of course he had – and thought he recognized an opportunity, an opportunity best taken advantage of in a cooperative, decent, orderly fashion. No

violence, no scramble. That's the nub of Don's approach. I
endorse it, of course.'

'Well, OK,' Margaret said. 'Thanks very much. We do
appreciate your position. Forgive the slight frostiness you
thought you might have detected earlier on. We see that as
regrettable now, I assure you, felt by both Ralph and myself.
I'd like the rough edges smoothed away. Great to have seen
you on our home ground, clearly special.'

'There is room, surely, for cooperation,' Chail said.

'Not so much "room",' Donald said. 'There is a need.'

'Yes, an obligation,' Chail said. 'This is what has brought
Donald and me here together, Ralph.'

'We have time,' Donald said. 'Given the state of things
generally, we still have time to make a move towards
takeover.'

'If we make our move *now*,' Chail said. 'Believe me, Ralph,
I am very aware of a breach of . . . well . . . protocol in our
rolling up here unannounced, but it's a matter of the
circumstances.'

'I share that awareness, though I'm from another region,'
Donald said.

'But it's to do with speed. Imperative,' Chail said.

They were standing in a circle, with Ralph nearest to the
Low Pastures front door. He couldn't recall having made a
deliberate effort to ensure that was how the positions worked
out. He thought it very correct, though, and very natural. The
fact that he had not worked to give it that shape, just accepted
it as deeply apt, satisfied him warmly. If he wanted to lead
them all in, he could do it as a sort of inevitable move, like
a corporal at a changing-of-the-guard ceremony.

Donald was next on the left of Ralph, then Margaret and
Chail. This meant that Chail was facing into the circle
and towards Ralph. He approved this. It looked as if Chail
realized it would be a gross mistake for him to believe he was
the one who should start a progress towards the Low Pastures
open door. His back was to the house and Ralph felt there
was a submissive gaze towards him by Chail, an appeal
to Ralph to cater for the next arrangement. Margaret was
alongside the old Peugeot and Ralph disliked that.

Ralph felt that any stranger looking in over the front lawns at the house would find the sight of the little group very comforting and sturdy, say like Bridge players breaking up after a session. Of course, that observer would not realize how crucial it was to note where each of the four was standing in relation to the others.

Ralph didn't play Bridge, but was fond of the notion of it, and meant to learn the game and join a club once he was not so busy. People often remarked on his inscrutability, when he wanted to be inscrutable, and he knew this would be an asset at Bridge. He could, though, certainly get rid of inscrutability on occasions under the hedge and similar lovely emotional joinings. Ralph had an idea people would guess that the very restrained aspect of Ralph often on show was not the total story. Most probably they would not be shocked to find them close under a bonny hedge, with Ralph really expressing himself.

He might suggest to Margaret that she should join a Bridge club with him. He had to be careful: Ralph thought she was possibly cleverer than he was and that could become evident in a Bridge game. He might not look just deadpan but thick.

'We recognize, naturally, Ralph, that you cannot regard this as the full expression of what it's all about,' Bernie Chail said.

'Excuse me. What *what* is all about?' Margaret said.

'Perhaps you feel that despite our grouping, there's one massive omission from our presentation,' Chail said.

'Manse,' Donald said. 'He ought to be here, shouldn't he?'

'Well, we've taken care of that,' Chail said. 'We were sure you'd agree to the invitation, Ralph, so we've asked him over. He had things to do but he'll join us in a little while.'

'That will help create a welcome completion,' Donald said, 'a fine fullness and strength.'

Ralph felt amazed by the rapidity and boldness of what he heard. It was almost impossible for him to swallow these proposals and assumptions. God! They thought they could invite a guest to Low Pastures. True, the guest was a prospective close business contact, but not someone Ralph frequently allowed into his property. He felt he must grab back his status as host. 'May I propose we go inside – a drink or at least

some tea and a sit-down.' He moved forward and then stood
politely to one side and let Margaret go ahead. Ralph went
next and then the other two. Ralph could not remember a time
when people from a car as drab as that Peugeot went into Low
Pastures' main front door regardless.

With a quick, decisive shuffle, Ralph took over the leadership of the little group from Margaret once they were into the
house. Enough politeness. She'd understand. He thought
the TV room with its hefty leather armchairs and a settee
would be right for the meeting, if he thought anywhere in the
property could be right, which, of course, he didn't: he was
caught in a kind of hold-up.

He tried to get rid of the idea in his head that the occasion
was symbolic. What it was was a couple of next-to-nothing
nobodies being shown a lot more tolerance than they could
have expected, unless they were powered by egomaniac greed.
But this they were, weren't they – intruders getting treated
with some elementary humanity. They were visitors to someone's home – admittedly an exceptional home, Ralph W.
Ember's, still a properly operational family haven. They were
not by any means welcome visitors, but presumptuous, devious,
arrogant visitors, but that was all. They were not a kind of
message that the glorious Ember business era was nearing its
end, or had already ended.

In fact, though, Ralph had only poor luck in his attempt to
keep things at a basic workaday level. He had known this
was probably how it would be. He was Ralph W. Ember, yes,
and Ralph W. Ember on his home patch, enclosed in excellent
leather, but Ralph W. Ember didn't necessarily control the
talk.

He thought they looked wrong for this superlative furniture.
That didn't make them blame-worthy. Many would have this
shortcoming, male or female. They sat on the settee and chair
as if they knew this was something temporary. Ralph felt that
the way an arse accosted a seat cushion would tell you things.
They were nervy. Ralph could sympathize with them. He,
personally, hadn't always been able to afford substantial
leather.

Chail sat alone on the settee, the others and Ralph in

armchairs. 'Shall I tell you what this is all about?' Margaret said with a terrific, commanding grin.

Chail uttered a tiny whoop of pleasure. 'I told Don, didn't I, Don?'

'You said Mrs Ember would give a verdict, perhaps an unexpected one. She would grasp at once the way things are. You said she had that sort of mind,' Don replied.

'I'd never met her until today, but the word about her is around and all of it of a similar flavour: positive, full of admiration, favourable to a remarkable degree – envious, much of it.'

'This visit is to do with Iles, isn't it?' Margaret said. 'To do with Desmond Iles.'

'Of course it is,' Chail said.

'Huge changes likely,' Don said.

'A certainty,' Chail said.

'This is going to become like a different country. OK, I'm from another area, but I feel the tension here already, the expectancy,' Don said. 'Perhaps it takes an outsider to register the vast pending change.'

'And that means there's space for all sorts of new developments in this city,' Chail said.

'Sweetly affecting you and your companies, for instance?' Margaret said, the grin as big as ever, but not a matey smile, a warning grin.

Chail smiled: 'I know you'll have had over the years a lot of approaches like this,' he said. His was a seeming congratulatory smile.

'By the thousand,' Margaret replied.

Chail nodded: it was more congratulation, as it were.

'And you've turned them away,' Chail said.

'By the same thousands,' Margaret said, grinning. 'They had nothing like enough to offer in exchange for our cooperation.'

'You'd be making a formidable demand, as is totally understandable,' Chail said, 'and it remains just as understandable today.'

'Absobloodylutely,' Donald said.

'But, yes, we can meet that demand,' Chail said.

'Absobloodylutely again,' Donald said.

'We wouldn't be troubling you if we did not believe that of ourselves,' Chail replied. 'No, if we didn't think that what we would like to propose is certain to benefit you as much as us. There's a difference now from those other approaches that you've had, a major difference, isn't there?'

'Flux,' Don said, 'to put it mildly.'

'You'll see this very clearly, I'm sure, Mrs Ember, and you as well, Ralph.'

'I don't want to play guessing games,' Ember said.

'No, that won't be necessary.' Chail paused, grew weighty. 'The difference between then and now is the total disappearance soon from this patch of Desmond Iles – his complete removal.' He paused again, obviously to let this register fully on the Embers.

'Yes,' Ralph replied, 'he's got another posting. It's promotion.'

'It's so much more than that,' Chail said.

'Much, much,' Don said.

'This is our gorgeous opportunity. It has to be grabbed and grabbed by us,' Bernie said. 'We have to crush potential rivals. It's sad in a way that Iles felt he had to go, but for us it's above all a positive. I'm talking merger, one brilliantly adept company – you, Ralph, Manse, Donald and myself, plus, of course, Mrs Ember, Margaret, should she wish that. Or perhaps you'll object and say although Iles might be on his way, his sidekick, Harpur, will still be with us. True, but Desmond Iles is an assistant chief. That's a very big rank – and he's going to something bigger, of course, because he is known by others to have those unique qualities and is willing to transplant them. An ACC deals with policy. He or she has stature. Iles has enormous presence here. But I don't have to tell you this. Harpur has rank as well, I'll admit. It's not in the same division as an ACC's, though. Iles has splendidly helped hold matters together in these parts. It's a kind of magic. Harpur's not up to that. Simply, he hasn't got it. He doesn't need to feel bad about that. Hardly anyone has.

'When Iles goes, his inborn skill at policy creation and preservation go with him. Chaos looms. I've seen it happen elsewhere, though not on the scale it would strike here, because a gap left by Iles can't be equalled – he is unmatched and a vast loss.

'But we note in the sand and gravel wharf murder what might actually be the beginnings of the coming disintegration, and that was only on account of rumour saying Desmond Iles *might* go. We know now it's definite. We're on the edge of break-up. We must get together, coalesce to make up for his otherwise disastrous absence. At this point I'd like to say a word about my friend, Donald. He is new to you, Mrs Ember, and to you, Ralph – other than those couple of minutes in the arcade. Don is a great student of the markets, and particularly our type of market, naturally. Because he saw very early on what was happening here, and what was due to happen, he dropped his other interests and got in touch with me. He did considerable research into our businesses, and into me.'

Chail smiled another good smile. 'Don discovered I'd become a dad and he reasoned, accurately enough, that my living costs were about to soar! Our new company will help deal with that for me, and things will be similar for you, Ralph.'

'I have a proper business plan at home for our marvellous amalgamated firm,' Donald said. 'I've put in an option depending on whether you, Margaret Ember, would like to take a directorship, and we'll keep a place ready and warm for that growing member of the Chail family, Egret.'

'Thank you, Don,' Chail said.

Margaret waved a finger, like reproaching a child. 'Very nicely expressed and thank you so much, Donald, for giving me an option on something that's never going to exist. I couldn't accept it, even if it did. Your business plan? Shite,' she said. 'What we have here is something Ralph and Manse Shale have lovingly created and nurtured. It is a feature of wonderful and enduring balance. We can't have it disturbed. Other dealers realize that they have to stay comparatively small-time, not much above negligible.

'Iles's departure doesn't affect the situation. His replacement here as ACC will be briskly but gently guided to the same sensible, decent arrangement. To be blunt, Chail, there's no room for you, or you, Donald. It would be lunacy on our part to allow any change and to take part in it. I'm amazed that you have the gall to propose this.'

It was the kind of reaction Ralph might have expected from her – might have, but hadn't quite. He recognized a bravery and audaciousness about it totally beyond him. That could happen sometimes with Margaret.

Ralph saw Don was infuriated by her words, especially the rubbishing of his business plan. He seemed to have been expecting automatic acceptance of his ideas and of him. Don stood, levering himself up from the arms of the leather chair, and seemed about to attack Margaret with a punch, battering or strangling to shut her up physically. That benign early glut of smiling stuff on their arrival meant nothing. The tone of moderation earlier meant nothing. The modest, grubby Peugeot was intended to get Ralph's guard down and suggest mildness, harmlessness. Don glanced at Chail who gave a small nod, perhaps permission for the brutality. Maybe among Don's attributes violence was included.

Urgently, Ralph also stood, ready to defend Margaret. As he straightened, though, he found himself slipping into that robot-like, stupid, useless gesture – the pocket tapping in ludicrous search for the gun that was not there, though suddenly needed.

But Donald was an outsider. He did not know about Ralph's rampant distaste these days for handguns, nor about Ralph's barmy, subconscious link to past habits. After only a couple of seconds, Ralph stopped the movement towards the imagined gun as he invariably did, but, very interestedly, he saw it was too late. Donald, obviously determined to defend himself, pulled out in a slick, quick action, what Ralph recognized as a Modelo automatic from a shoulder holster and was turning to blast Ralph when there erupted the booming crackle of a four-shot salvo from near the door of the room and Don, close to Margaret, slowly bent double where he was and fell helplessly, the beard soaked in blood and dripping on to his fine-quality shoes. Manse Shale came forward, stiff right arm pointing a Smith & Wesson pistol at Donald, inert on the ground, and kicked the Modelo away. Manse had on a grey pinstripe three-piece suit with fob-watch pocket waistcoat and gold chain, brown Ascot trilby, and radiantly white shirt with cutaway collar and plain, purple tie.

'You OK, Ralph?' Manse said. 'That's what I call timing. Wouldn't you say so? I gathered it was something special and decided I'd better dress properly. This is the kind of person I am, isn't it Ralph? You can vouch for that. I like to harmonize with my surroundings, but if those surroundings are a mess, as with the bearded dead one here, then I feel compulsion to correct the circumstances, restore serenity and true order. This wasn't exactly the kind of special situation I expected, so a bit of adaptation was required. Chail, you can bugger off and don't come back, ever. Your surname is too much like mine in sound and I'd hate to get mixed up with you. Think yourself lucky. Things are going to stay beautifully the same here. True, we'll feel the absence of Mr Iles for a while, but the incomer will soon see the splendour of what the ACC has created – with, of course, the partnership strength of Detective Chief Harpur, and this successor to Mr Iles will be glad to carry matters forward in the individual style brought to us by our assistant chief (Operations).'

TWENTY-TWO

Harpur and Iles were in Harpur's office again for one of their special character-building chats. Iles said: 'I don't think Manse will go to jail for long, if at all. He acted fast to save a life, didn't he, Ralph Ember's; or that's what he thought and how they'll plead in court. The fact that Mansel Shale is a widower could make a jury feel sympathetic. He might avoid prison altogether. Possession of firearm? But without a firearm he might not have been able to save a life. That's how his case could be presented. It's convincing, it's virtually true.'

'Ralph has let it be known that he and his wife would be prepared to look after Manse's daughter if he was given a clink sentence,' Harpur said.

Iles said: 'I heard this too. It's very much in keeping with the way matters are conducted here. I'll miss that sweetness and light, Col.'

There were definite times when Iles seemed wonderfully and benignly in touch with the core of the community he served, and with humanity in general.

Harpur had the secret opinion that Iles would have liked to be permanently of that refreshing nature but hadn't got there yet. No, a good way off yet.

'At times like this I tend to think of the well-known French poet, Col.'

'Ah, yes,' Harpur said. 'I had an idea you'd be mulling along those lines, sir.'

'Which?' Iles said.

'Which lines? Those from the French poet,' Harpur said.

'They can put their finger pretty decisively on matters over there.'

'Which matters are those, sir?'

'Life. Its aspects.'

'Ah.'

'The poet looks around him and is not too pleased at what he sees,' Iles said.

'I believe that would be true of most poets,' Harpur replied. '"Jack and Jill". Here's another cracked head. There'd be plenty of rhymes for those two.'

'The poet I have in mind, Col . . .'

'The French one?' Harpur said.

'This poet, de Musset asks us, the readers, if we like it here.'

'Here being where, sir?' Harpur replied.

'Not just here in the town or area,' Iles said. 'The world, the planet. I've heard others quote these lines.'

'That's quite a topic,' Harpur said.

'The poet wants to know whether we regret not being here when things were so different, as if the gods were on the downside with us, not up there in the heavens.'

'I believe I can see what you're getting at, sir.'

'"*Je suis venu trop tard dans un monde trop vieux*",' Iles said. '"I've turned up too late in a world that's too old".'

'Denise is doing French at the university and has to go to France for a year. She'll be able to translate that sort of stuff,' Harpur said, 'no problem.'

'My answer to the poet, Col, is obviously, "Yes, I am out of tune with where we are. I want somewhere else. I have a longing for that." The poet longed for the fabled past. Impossible. I'm stuck with the future – northern cops. Exciting? I wonder.'

'The gods are not on call to give you a choice,' Harpur said.

'I'll probably withdraw.'

'From the new chiefdom?' Harpur said.

'It would be a nothing move. The same, only different.'

'The poet would probably back you.'

'Sarah would as well, you two-timing sod.'

TWENTY-THREE

C hief Inspector Francis Garland thought the wharf casualty had been executed by an outsider, specifically Donald Om, but he was dead and not available for questions. He might have regarded the freelance as dangerous competition. Rebecca had gone back to London.

As a result, Harpur had some periods of time with which to do what he liked, and he looked in on Manse Shale's trial for murder. The trial was spread over several days, partly because the judge wanted to visit Low Pastures to see where the shooting took place. Iles had said Manse might get off. Harpur wondered, though. It disturbed him that the prosecution department had insisted on a murder charge, not manslaughter or something less. Harpur thought it would be bad if Manse were removed from the scene for years, bad for the scene as well as Manse. Likewise, in a way, if Iles went. The ACC had withdrawn from the northern posting partly because he thought his removal would put the sweetness and light of this region in peril if he left. Of course, Iles would not acknowledge this as a reason for his change of mind. He'd regard such a statement as pompous, soft, egomaniacal. Iles *was* egomaniacal, but he hated being caught out openly showing it.

Iles had called up that French poetic twaddle to provide him with an excuse for his decision to exit. Harpur had told Denise about the fairytale French, and she'd said that if Iles wanted an inspiration, he should go to another nineteenth-century French poem called 'The Death of the Wolf'. And the wolf says, 'Do your long and heavy duty, then snuff it without complaint.'

Harpur considered that both Iles and Manse were needed to protect and cherish the domestic heartland whose placid charms they had helped create. The consciousness of this was what made Iles turn down the new job.

On all of Harpur's visits to the trial, Shale, in the dock, seemed relaxed, his voice strong. He was facing the judge, of course, so Harpur in the public seats behind had only occasional sight of Manse's profile when he half-turned to look around the courtroom. Harpur wasn't sure whether Manse had glimpsed him. He gave no sign. A woman guard was seated with him in the dock. He'd been in jail on remand. Twice when Harpur thought Shale might be aware of him he tried a few winks. These might not have got through to him though.

The prosecuting lawyer was keen to establish the setting for the crime correctly and the number of people involved. He described the group as 'four becoming five' in a ground-floor room in a house known as Low Pastures.

'Yes,' Manse said.

The lawyer asked Shale to name the four for the jury.

Manse said they were Mr Ralph Ember, Mrs Margaret Ember, Mr Bernard Chail and Mr Donald Om.

'Low Pastures is the home of Mr and Mrs Ember, isn't it?' the lawyer said.

'Yes.'

'Why had this group come together in Low Pastures on that afternoon?'

'Social occasion.'

'What sort of social occasion?'

'Social.'

'Was it a planned social occasion?'

'How do you mean, planned?'

'Arranged in advance,' the QC said.

'In advance of what?' Manse said.

'Or had they just dropped in when passing by?'

'I don't know.'

'Very well. But you were there by arrangement, weren't you?'

'I don't remember.'

'A grey pinstripe suit,' the lawyer said. 'Do you own a grey pinstripe suit?'

'I think so,' Manse said.

'You have a lot of suits, do you?'

'Not a lot. More than one,' Shale said.

'The one the court is interested in is a three-piece suit. That is, it has a waistcoat.'

'I think one of them has a waistcoat.'

'This waistcoat has a fob pocket, doesn't it? And there was a silver chain leading from it to the other pocket.'

'Could be,' Mansel said.

'It's a very impressive outfit, isn't it?' the QC said. 'There's an Ascot-style trilby and a very well-laundered and -pressed white shirt with cutaway collar.'

'I'm in favour of smart white collars.'

'The whole ensemble was exceptionally smart, wasn't it?'

'I like to give some attention to my appearance. Members of the Bar need to be well-dressed, I understand,' Shale said. 'I heard that a judge stated that he couldn't hear a lawyer who was dressed in a leather jacket. That didn't mean he couldn't hear him – nothing wrong with his ears – but he wouldn't listen to him.'

'Quite so,' the lawyer said. 'You spoke of this at the time, didn't you? One of the other members of the group made a note of it. You said you'd guessed there was something special due, and you'd better dress accordingly.'

'Did I?'

'It wasn't just a social occasion, was it?'

'Wasn't it?'

The prosecution lawyer was still working on Manse when Harpur and Iles next looked in on the trial.

'Why did you think it necessary to take a .38 Smith and Wesson?' the QC asked. 'A popular gun.'

'These are dangerous times,' Shale replied.

'But you said you were merely going to a meeting with friends, didn't you, what you called a social occasion.'

'I didn't know all of them very well.'

'What was the friendship with Bernard Chail and Ralph Ember based on?'

'Business,' Shale said.

'What kind of business?'

'Various.'

'Drugs?' the QC said.

'Various,' Manse said.

'Drug dealing can be a very violent occupation, can't it?' the QC said.

'I believe so,' Shale said.

'Did you take the pistol with you because you feared you might have to defend yourself?'

'As I've said, these are dangerous times.'

'So you did think you might have to defend yourself?'

'This city and the area around it are for the most part peaceful and safe,' Shale said.

'So why did you take the gun?'

'Sometimes order breaks down, even in the best places,' Shale said.

'But were you part of that breakdown? Did you join them at Low Pastures because you intended to kill one of them with the .38 pistol?' The lawyer wanted to prove intent. That could make it murder.

'No,' Manse replied.

When the defence took over, Harpur at once had the feeling that Iles, sitting alongside him again in the public area, considered Shale's QC was making a fuck-up of things. 'The bastard's pussyfooting,' Iles whispered, not very quietly, to Harpur. 'Where's his grand indignation and disbelief that his guiltless client should be put through this disgusting victimization?'

A court attendant, trudging gingerly, approached Iles, gesturing with a hand to his lips that Iles should tone it down. 'Piss off,' the ACC said at just-under-normal voice.

'Tell the jury would you please, Mr Shale, why you decided you must shoot the guest you knew as Donald?'

'I thought he was about to attack Mr Ralph Ember.'

'Why did you think that?'

'Mrs Ember, Ralph's wife, had said something that deeply offended Donald and Mr Bernard Chail. I wasn't present for what she said but was told what it was later. I hadn't arrived until some moments after what Mrs Ember had spoken about. I knew only that there was acute and very dangerous tension in the room. I saw Donald produce a gun and seem to threaten Ralph with it. Ralph had taken a position to protect his wife.

I feared that Donald would fire at Mr or Mrs Ember or both as a kind of response to what she had said. I had to act very quickly to annul Donald Om, and as I stood in the doorway of the room I fired at him using four shots so as to be certain,' Shale said.

'In other words, this was a measure to save Mr and Mrs Ember from harm on their own property?'

'Yes.'

'Was this incident planned?'

'No, how could it be? I couldn't know what had taken place to cause this crisis.'

'Would you please tell the jury why you were carrying a gun?'

'It was illegal, but I had reason to think that the Low Pastures mansion was the site of recent abnormal events. I wanted to be able to defend myself.'

'And you guarded someone else, didn't you?' the lawyer said.

'I was glad to do it.'

'You had not planned a killing, had you? There was no intent?' the lawyer said. 'Thank you, Mr Shale.'

Iles didn't hang about when the trial ended but went home in a continuing rage at how the defence had run things. He was not present to hear the unanimous not guilty verdict on all charges. Harpur did stay long enough to give Shale a thumbs-up when he appeared in the road. He had on his own clothes, not remand garb, but nothing too fruity.

TWENTY-FOUR

In the late afternoon, Harpur drove Hazel, Jill and Denise to the airport. Denise was flying to Grenoble, France, to start her year's residence as part of her degree. The girls and Harpur were there to see her off. 'We'll all miss you,' Hazel said.

'But Dad the most,' Jill said.

'Naturally,' Hazel replied.